"You are a wonderful person," Greg continued.

"I'd just like to see you do something out of the ordinary, something impulsive."

She whirled around and, with remarkably good aim, smashed the pie directly into Greg's face. She pulled back her hand, and the tin pie plate stuck for a moment before sliding off and hitting the floor with a muffled clatter.

Greg blinked and his eyes appeared in the middle of the mess.

"I didn't mean to do that," Jane gasped. "I don't know. . . I just. . . You said. . ."

Greg licked his lips.

"That's a start. That was certainly unexpected." He licked his lips again, and she could see the grin.

"I'm so sorry," she said, grabbing the towel hanging from the ring beside the sink. He caught her hand before she could wipe off the evidence of her spontaneity.

"Oh no you don't," he exclaimed. "Now you must receive retribution." His voice alerted her to some plan that she would most likely find disagreeable.

"What are you thinking?" she asked.

"Revenge." He took hold of her other wrist and backed her against the counter.

"What are you going to do?"

"Share."

KATHLEEN PAUL lives in Colorado Springs. Retired from teaching, she gets that weekly dose of kids she needs to keep going by being a storyteller in the Sunday school department of her church. During the week, she leads two workshops for Christian writers. Her life is full, with an eighty-five-year-old mom in residence to keep her in line, two grown children to keep her active, and three dogs to keep her laughing.

HEARTSONG PRESENTS

Out in
the Real World

Kathleen Paul

Heartsong Presents

To my family and friends who make my Real World wonderful.

A note from the author:
I love to hear from my readers! You may correspond with me
by writing: **Kathleen Paul**
Author Relations
PO Box 719
Uhrichsville, OH 44683

ISBN 1-58660-320-5

OUT IN THE REAL WORLD

Cover illustration by Jocelyne Bouchard.

PRINTED IN THE U.S.A.

one

"So you see, Miss Freedman, my father's not interested in a romantic entanglement. He's still devoted to my mother's memory. She was the one Great Love of his life."

The melodramatic tones of the teen coaxed a smile to the lips of the twenty-six-year-old interior designer. It hovered and died before it completely lifted the corners of her mouth. This whole episode held an undertone of sadness.

A booth at Mike's Midtown Burgers during the noon rush hour just didn't seem the right setting for this young lady's theatrical utterances. Jane Freedman studied her young companion a moment and then carefully looked away.

The background looked real enough. Chattering people filled each of the round tables. More sat tucked away in the booths lining the room. Waitresses wove between the tables balancing trays of hamburgers and French fries, chicken strips, onion rings, and soda in tall paper cups with straws bobbing between the ice cubes. The unmistakable odor of deep-fry wafted through the air. Rock music pulsed an accompaniment to the clatter of dishes and jingle of change at the register.

Jane shook herself hoping she'd wake up from some inexplicable dream. Her short mass of dark brown curls shivered and settled back down into a disheveled cap. Closing her eyes for a moment to shut out the scene around her, she fervently wished she had declined the unusual invitation to lunch. Opening her eyes and shifting her attention to her companion, she sighed. The serious face of thirteen-year-old Amy Boskell convinced her of the reality in this bizarre situation. Jane wasn't quite sure whether to laugh at the girl's presumption or cry for her.

Amy straightened her petite form. "And," she continued, "my mother's *twin* sister takes care of nurturing the family, so we don't need another mother. We are *all* quite content as we are."

The young lady speaking seemed perfectly confident in her words. The only hint of nervousness was her inability to meet the older woman's eyes.

She's short, thought Jane absurdly. *One mustn't laugh at short people or people who are making fools of themselves. It isn't kind.*

The preposterous stray thought reestablished Jane's sense of balance. It put distance between her and the girl. This was only an extraordinary incident, nonintrusive upon her stable life. She could watch the scene almost as if it were a play, a poorly written play. At least, she could try. She wasn't going to be called upon to do anything. Over the years, God had given her peace when there was none. Surely He wouldn't use this child to destroy her peace. She still had the option to walk away.

Jane's honey-colored silk suit had a spattering of crumbs across the front. She carefully took her paper napkin and brushed them away. She'd be returning to work soon, and a specialized interior designer had an image to upkeep. Bits and pieces of your lunch did not count as fashionable accessories.

"I think perhaps you misunderstand the nature of your father's interest in me," Jane began cautiously. "We have had two *business* dinners. Three clients were present, and we discussed the next steps in the renovation of the Baker estate."

"My father's a very warm and friendly man, Miss Freedman," said Amy earnestly. "I don't want you to misinterpret his intentions. I don't want you to get hurt. He would *never* take another wife, unless maybe my aunt Kate could be persuaded to marry him."

Where did this child get such outrageous notions and the gall to act upon them? Jane shook her head slowly from side to side in amazement. Never had she encountered such a situation, and she wasn't quite sure how to deal with this cool teenager.

Amy Boskell sat across the orange Formica and chrome table sipping the straw of her soda. Amy portrayed haphazard brand-name insensibility. Her jeans and tight-fitting knit shirt looked exactly like the outfits on four other girls in the burger shop. Red hair parted precisely in the middle hung down to the jawbone framing the pixie face. Serious green eyes looked out through the wire-framed glasses. Amy took one finger and pushed the bridge of the glasses up on her nose.

Jane dragged her mind back to the moment at hand. Hadn't she read in some article a viewpoint deploring the next generation maturing far too rapidly? She'd only skimmed the article in a waiting room. After all, she wasn't prescient and hadn't known she'd be cornered by an adolescent within weeks.

The maturation of any child wasn't likely to be one of Jane's areas of concern. The youngest of her siblings, she'd never baby-sat. Early in her miserable childhood, she determined to stay out of the family scene forever. Families weren't worth the trouble.

Given her lack of experience with any children and her determined disinterest, it was not surprising that this child/woman had caught her off guard. Trying to grasp some handle on this situation, she cast around for an identifying trait of this teenager. It worked in dealing with clients. Greg Boskell's daughter had an extensive vocabulary and a lot of self-confidence for her age. Did that help? No.

Well, it really wasn't any of her business. She'd accepted the invitation to lunch out of curiosity. Now that she knew what was on the girl's mind, she could only do her best to reassure her and leave it at that.

Reassure her. Now that was odd. Why had that phrase popped up in her mind?

Surely this self-possessed young lady doesn't need an outsider like me to reassure her about anything. Why do I have this nagging feeling that this girl is crying out for help? Absurd. Jane firmly repeated to herself, *This is none of my business.*

"We go on quite famously," Amy continued, and Jane thought, *That sounds like a line from an old movie, or a book.*

"My aunt doesn't live with us, of course, but she works from our home, so she's there when we go off to school and when we come home. When my father comes home, she leaves. She lives with my Grandmother and Grandfather Standish."

Grandmother, Grandfather, not Grandma and Grandpa. What's with this kid?

Jane sipped her iced tea and made no comment.

"Dad enjoys her company, of course. Kate's company." Amy added by way of explanation and dipped a French fry into catsup. "She doesn't like us to call her Aunt Kate. We're friends as well as relatives. Of course, Dad enjoys Grandmother's company as well."

Of course, thought Jane. *"As well" must be her phrase of the week.*

"They sometimes go out for dinner. Kate and Dad, not Grandmother. To talk, you know. They're very attracted to each other, but Mother's like a ghost between them." Amy sighed dramatically. Jane fought the urge to roll her eyes.

This really is bizarre. Jane checked her watch, hoping time had leapt somehow and she could legitimately claim she had to rush off to some meeting, any meeting.

Amy waved another French fry dripping with catsup and continued, "Of course, Dad hasn't had any sex since Mother died, and—"

Jane choked on her tea and felt her mask of indifference slip as her eyes widened.

"Wait a minute, Amy," Jane objected. "I hardly think that your father's personal life is a suitable topic of conversation between us."

"Oh, you must realize that teenagers of today understand a lot more about sex than any previous generation."

The child blinked cool, sophisticated eyes. Jane swallowed the nerve-induced lump in her throat. *She's probably enjoying my discomfort,* thought Jane. She hardened her face into another mask before she turned her attention back to the girl's words.

"I only wanted you to know that even though my father may be physically lonely, his spiritual and emotional needs are well met."

"Sorry, Amy, but this conversation is making me extremely uncomfortable. I enjoyed the lunch, but I must get back to the office." *How dare this kid speak so. . .* The word wouldn't come to her mind, and Jane felt frustration bubbling in her chest. *Children should not be allowed out like this.* "Don't you have school today?" she snapped.

"No, today is a teachers' workday. And the little children are with Grandmother Standish."

"Little children?"

"My little brothers and sister."

"Oh." Jane struggled with what to say. "I don't know how many children are in your family."

Amy smiled and for the first time looked directly at her lunch partner.

Man, does this daddy have his work cut out for him, thought Jane. *Why does Amy Boskell look so pleased with herself? Has she accomplished whatever her purpose was for this lunch? Well, if there is another invitation, I'll arrange to be busy.* She signaled for the waitress to bring the tab.

"This is my treat," said Amy firmly. "It was my invitation."

Jane looked the girl over once again. How had such odd and fragmentary adult attitudes been trapped in this small body? If anything, Amy Boskell looked immature for her age. Thin, with an exaggerated straight posture, her shoulders just cleared the booth's table. Her conversation belied the little girl appearance. The way she spoke, the ideas she expressed, were precocious, not infantile.

"Would you like me to cover the tip, then?" offered Jane.

A flash of uncertainty crossed the elfin face, but with a shake of her head it was gone.

"No. Thank you for coming." Her plastic smile and determined eyes held no warmth. "It was a pleasure to chat with you."

Jane said her thanks for the lunch and good-bye and beat a hasty retreat. This small being who passed for an adolescent made her nervous.

She stepped outside into the cool air of Colorado's November and hailed a cab. She might not be the brightest woman in the world, but she was smart enough to get out of the water when she couldn't swim.

Jane Freedman jumped into the cab and gave the address of her temporary office. She couldn't get away from Mike's Midtown Burgers fast enough.

Well, curiosity killed the cat, she thought. *Now maybe I'll curb my curiosity next time I'm tempted.*

The last half hour left her with a churning stomach and it wasn't Mike's famous Mighty Burger that did it. She leaned back against the rough upholstery of the cab's backseat and closed her eyes. The scent of dust and age, a musty blend of thousands of past passengers and the cab's own history assaulted her. But she couldn't keep the image of petite and strange Amy Boskell from harassing her thoughts.

Yes, strange is the right word. Surely all teenagers aren't so intense. Why did she pick on me?

Jane opened her eyes and took note of the downtown Denver street full of people hurrying to wherever they had to be on their lunch hour.

They didn't have a burger and fries with a psycho. Well, psycho is a bit harsh, admitted Jane as she mused over the unusual call she'd had from a client's daughter. *Maybe I am a little attracted to Greg Boskell and that's why I accepted.*

That was then and this is now. Greg Boskell has suddenly grown another head and looks like a monster to me. Thanks, Amy, for pushing me back from a big mistake.

two

"Jane Freedman."

Jane turned in the church aisle to see who had called her name. She was visiting in this church for the first time. How extraordinary that she would run across someone she knew when she knew so few people in Denver.

She smiled when she saw the tall man in the trim-fitting gray suit working his way through the aisle full of people. Greg Boskell's rather ordinary-looking face became animated in conversation and changed him from plain to interesting. He had a good face to watch as he talked. His eyebrows were mobile, and during business meetings last winter she had been distracted upon several occasions just observing their antics. He had what Jane had decided was a Mickey Mouse smile. It didn't sound flattering, but a certain quirk to it reminded her of the cartoon character's ageless charm—thin lips with a mischievous grin lurking perpetually at the corners.

Thank goodness he didn't have the squeaky voice to match. Instead, he had what she had once heard referred to as a bedroom voice when a movie critic described an actor's throaty delivery. She chose a different description. It sounded deep and rough as if he'd just come in from yelling all afternoon to root his team on for a fantastic win.

Jane found him personable and she enjoyed working with him. Their mutual client had been a tad temperamental. Greg tactfully brought down some of the woman's more outrageous expectations to reasonable levels. For that, Jane owed him a debt of gratitude.

It had been ten months since her business trip to Denver. Now her boss had moved her division to the area, and she was just settling in. It was good to see a familiar face.

At that moment the crowd parted and a not-so-friendly face scowled at her. Amy Boskell.

Oh, Jane groaned inwardly. *I'd forgotten the formidable teen. Of course she isn't happy to see her father eagerly greeting me.*

Even from clear across the sanctuary Jane could feel Amy's hostility.

Greg Boskell smiled down at Jane and took the hand she had automatically extended, claiming her attention at the same time. They shook and he pulled her off to the side a little, letting the congregation file out past them.

"What are you doing in Denver? Are you on another buying trip for Mark?" he asked.

She shook her head. "Mark's moved the Western division to Denver, and that means me and three others. He said it made more sense than constantly sending his buyers halfway across the continent. He's also opening a showroom. Actually, I cover West and Southwest, but not California. California rates its own department."

"I didn't realize Mark's business was so complicated. I mean, it's basically interior decorating, isn't it?"

"Technically, when you spend all that time in school and gain a few years' experience, you're allowed to be a little smug and refer to it as interior design." She smiled pleasantly, not offended that someone else questioned just what in the world she did for Mark Banner's Designs in Antiquity. "It's more like the 'architecture of the interior.' I also find banisters and bathtubs from houses built a century ago to be installed in mansions mimicking days gone by. My job's a little more than picking the draperies and hanging pictures."

Greg nodded and looked over his shoulder. "My family will be swooping down on me in a minute. We generally gather in the foyer. It helps to have one spot to assemble. Saves me chasing kids all over the building."

"You have children," Jane stated, making sure she didn't imply a question. She knew he had children. Last winter she'd had lunch with one. "That didn't come up at our meetings."

"Yes." Greg steered her toward the foyer. "Four. Do you have a family?"

"Lots. But no husband, no kids."

"Over here by the potted plants. Jake calls it the forest."

As they passed through the doors from the sanctuary to the outer foyer, the ceiling rose to include the space adjacent to the second floor. Stain glass windows from floor to ceiling made up one wall, and clear glass doors made up another. Giant potted plants were clustered together in planters that doubled as benches. Some of the older members of the congregation sat around the small trees, waiting for their rides. Two boys played tag among the foliage.

"Jacob, Thomas, sit down." Greg called out. Immediately, the boys dove for a seat and succeeded in knocking each other on the floor. Greg descended upon them in a flash and stood them shoulder to shoulder. "You forgot," he said sternly. "There are older people here you could knock over. You may *not* play here while you're waiting for the rest of the family. Sit on the benches."

Greg turned to Jane and made the introductions. "These are my boys. Jake's five and Thomas is six. Here comes my daughter Caroline. Caroline, this is Miss Freedman. Caroline's eight and I have an older daughter, Amy. She's probably still visiting with her friends. Amy's my little adult."

Jane winced at the memory of his "little adult," but Greg didn't notice her expression.

Caroline shyly took her father's hand and, after a tiny nod acknowledging the introduction, she peered earnestly at Jane. The boys had given her the same cursory nod and then fell into a discussion of their own.

Jane smiled at the fair-haired girl.

"Hello, Caroline. Are you ready to go back to school? I understand from one of my clients that the school year begins this week."

"Yes, Ma'am." She had an enchanting smile. Freckles

spattered across a little snub nose. Soft, brown curls fluffed out around her head like a halo. Jane assumed the short haircut circumvented the challenge of getting a comb through those curls.

"We go out to eat every Sunday," said Greg. "It's tradition. A family restaurant. You're welcome to join us."

Jane could see Amy approaching behind her father. If there was one thing Jane did *not* want, it was to get mixed up with a family in the throes of mental illness. The child now wore a studied mask of innocence, but Jane had seen that face a moment earlier when the girl's thoughts blazed across her features like neon lights. Daddy was out-of-bounds for Jane.

Jane smiled as she uttered polite regrets. She had boxes to unpack. Her dog was waiting to be let out. Some other time. She escaped before being introduced to the daughter she'd already met.

ॐ

"Why don't you give that account to Bunny, Mark?"

Jane sat across from his desk with her lap covered. A notebook, her day planner, and two swatches of fabric they had been discussing balanced on her crossed legs.

"I thought you had time. Aren't you wrapping up with the Hendersons?" Mark looked briefly puzzled but went back to the sketch he held on a clipboard. He focused on it, penciled in a few lines, and missed Jane's reaction.

She rolled her eyes, thinking she'd best come up with a good excuse. How was she to go about explaining that she preferred not to be assigned any project that included working with Greg Boskell? Should she just calmly explain she suspected his daughter was a psychopath?

When there was no answer, Mark pulled his attention away from his project and leveled a stare at his best troubleshooter.

"What's up?"

Jane took a deep breath and plunged in. "I worked with Greg Boskell last year."

"Are you telling me he's a womanizer? Sexual harassment?"

"No, of course not," Jane quickly interjected.

"Well, that's good. I thought he was going to be one of our solid Christian connections in this city. I would've been disappointed."

Mark liked to deal with Christians whenever possible and to be a "shining witness" when it was not. He chose dedicated Christians to be his core employees. In many ways, it made working together a lot easier. Even so, at times these cherished Christian employees still acted like sinful people. Then, Mark's Christian-based negotiations between employees rubbing each other the wrong way did much to alleviate tense situations.

"Last year I got an invitation from his daughter Amy to meet for lunch," said Jane. "She warned me off her dad as if I were chasing him. She said that her father was perfectly content and didn't want a new wife."

"So, you found Greg attractive." A small grin tilted one corner of Mark's lips.

"No," exclaimed Jane. "It was all the daughter's imagination. It was really weird, Mark, and I don't want to be caught up in their problems. And Bunny, with her grandmother-type image, will be better handling the side issues in this case."

Sixty-year-old Bunny was wise and wonderful, funny and caring. Jane could not think of anyone better suited to handle the Boskell account, but she'd willingly suggest everyone else in the office, one by one, in order to avoid doing it herself.

"Maybe God isn't planning on another grandmother-type in the young lady's life." Mark raised his eyebrows in that aggravating way he had when he wanted his workers to be spiritual in their thinking. Jane hadn't noticed how irritating it was before, but now she felt like grabbing hold of the fuzzy lines in a nice strong pinch and bringing them back down to where they belonged.

"Mark," Jane continued in a carefully controlled voice, "I am totally unqualified as a teen counselor. Except for the unfortunate lunch with Amy Boskell, I haven't spoken two words together to a thirteen year old since I was one myself."

"Maybe God wants a Christian, not a counselor."

"Maybe God wants His trusted servant Mark to quit trying to second-guess Him."

Mark grinned. "Well, Jane, I'll see what I can do in the future, but Greg asked for you and I already said you were available." He turned back to his drawing. His fingers had been fidgeting with the unoccupied pencil.

Jane sighed, recognizing that to her boss the matter was settled. She bundled up the things in her lap to take back to her desk.

"How's Suggums?" Mark asked just as she juggled the load and tried to turn the handle of his office door.

"Suggums?"

"Yes, your pregnant dog, remember? She was one of your concerns about moving."

"She's fine." Jane smiled at the thought of her small companion. Suggums was a purebred Shih Tzu and every ounce a pampered dog. Jane had invested a lot of time in training her and now she was rewarded with an eager-to-please, undemanding, congenial, full-time confidante. "The trip didn't seem to bother her. I have an appointment with a local vet this Friday."

"Hmmm." His mind had gone back to his drawing, but he had not completely forgotten her. "You can work from your home if you need to play nursemaid to the mom and pups."

"Thanks, Mark." Jane shook her head as she left the room, quietly pulling the door shut behind her and almost dropping her load once more. Mark was a great boss, a pain to work for, and other times very considerate. Totally oblivious to the predicament at the door where she couldn't find the doorknob for fear of dropping her load, he hadn't offered to help. Yet what boss would understand that she wanted to be home with her new babies when they came?

As for the Boskell account, she didn't have much choice. She'd handle the situation as best she could, but she was *not* going to get involved with the family.

three

"These sketches look great, Jane." Greg handed her the portfolio across his office desk. She took it and opened her briefcase as he leaned back in his chair.

"So, do you like living in Colorado?" Greg asked.

Jane's lips pressed into a firm line. She didn't want to talk about her likes and dislikes. She just wanted to do her job and get out of his office. She took a steadying breath, concentrating on getting the folder into the right slot within her briefcase, stalling for time.

His tone was just friendly. Why did she always react as if he'd made a move on her? Why did she always feel it was necessary to throw up her walls of defense whenever they met? In the three weeks they'd been working on the Miller project, he had not once gone beyond the professional relationship. And she. . .well, to be honest, she had been *coldly* professional.

She shrugged, "I like the work. I haven't been here long enough to form an opinion of the area."

"I'm taking the kids up to Estes Park this weekend. Would you like to come along? It's called the Gateway to the Rockies and there's some fabulous scenery."

Jane tried a smile, tried to respond naturally to his offer like she would to any other adult, tried to sound unaffectedly friendly, tried to be humorous without being overly familiar. . . . Tried too hard and ended up sounding stiff again. "Your kids are into scenery?"

"No, they like to hike a little and shop a lot in the curio stores. Especially Amy. Amy takes after her mother in her artistic abilities. I'd like you to meet her. I think the type of interior design you do would appeal to her. Amy's truly a remarkable person."

17

We've already met, Sir. The answer came pouring into Jane's thoughts but she clamped down on the words before they reached her mouth.

"Well, thanks for the offer to join your family outing," Jane said aloud, "but I have to stay home with my dog."

"Stay home with your dog?" It did sound ridiculous echoed at her that way.

"Oh," said Jane, realizing how flimsy the excuse sounded. She did not want to hurt his feelings. He *was* a nice man. "She should whelp in the next day or two."

"Whelp?" He looked puzzled, then she saw the light dawn on his face. "Puppies."

"Yes, this is the second time she's been a mother, and I want to be there."

"Well, maybe some other time." Greg got up and stretched. "Mark told me you had left all your family to come work out here. I thought you might be lonely."

He smiled at her in that crooked, disarming way that she found wonderfully charming.

That's it, she said to herself. *I find him too attractive.*

"If there's one thing I have, it's enough family to share," he continued. "My crazy family keeps me sane."

A bombardment of conflicting thoughts caught Jane Freedman in a whirlwind. One surfaced above the others: This man's approach to his family was diametrically opposed to her own. She ignored the path this might lead her down and zeroed in on Mark's obvious interference. He'd told Greg she missed her family. What poppycock!

"I can't imagine why Mark told you that. It's misleading. I left my family with no regrets."

Jane watched Greg struggle to keep his expression neutral. She inwardly squirmed as she recognized his reaction. He was appalled that she blatantly disliked her relatives.

What do I care? Jane chastised herself. *I'm not supposed to care what he thinks.*

The attraction she felt for him was annoying, uncomfortable.

She certainly didn't want him attracted to her. The heightened awareness of his warm and generous personality was downright unpleasant. Jane was tired of the tingly, silly romantic feelings that overwhelmed her each time she came in contact with this man.

She'd successfully walled off any outside entanglements until this guy showed up. It was embarrassing that he managed to crumble her defenses and more embarrassing that he didn't seem to be aware of what he did to her. On second thought, if he did know, she would certainly die of embarrassment. It was all so juvenile.

She gathered up her things quickly.

She should just let him think she was an ogre, that her lack of affection for her family was a character fault. Maybe this volatile situation would defuse itself. She shoved her purse strap up on her shoulder and stood to leave, but her mouth opened on its own accord.

"They call it a dysfunctional family. I'm the only Christian, and I'm not welcome among them."

Her lips thinned in a line of disapproval. Her tongue, that wicked beast with a mind of its own, had betrayed her. She'd said more than she intended.

I don't owe him any explanations. He puts my peace of mind in jeopardy. I'd best get out of this room quickly, pronto, stat.

"I'm sorry." He reached to help her with her jacket.

"No, no need to be sorry." She cut him off. She grabbed her jacket. She wasn't about to put all this stuff down, struggle into the jacket, pick it all back up, and try to leave gracefully. She was just going to leave. "That's *really* ancient history. I moved out when I was fifteen and lived with an aunt."

"She was a Christian?"

"No, she was not." Better not go into Aunt's theology mixed with mysticism. Her freethinking regarding amorous partners. Her interest in herbs, crystals, and horoscopes.

"But, it was a comfortable situation?" the man persisted.

"No, it was not," she answered curtly.

"I'm sorry, Jane. I feel like I'm harassing you and I meant only to offer friendship." He truly sounded sincere.

"I don't need your friendship. I'm sure your life is busy enough raising four kids on your own."

This time he interrupted her.

"Do you really believe that?"

She looked puzzled. "Believe I don't need another friend-ship? That you're busy? Yes, and yes."

"No." He shook his head. "Believe that because I'm busy with my physical family, God doesn't allow me time to be friendly to someone in my spiritual family?"

She had no answer and just stared at him.

"You see, Jane, I was thinking that you *are* a member of my family." She still looked blankly at him. He continued in that warm, soft voice that did odd things to her toes. "You know, as in 'the church.' "

A man's voice should not physically affect one's toes. Jane tightened her jaw and her determination. She retreated to safe ground with all possible speed.

"I'll have the final proposal to you on Monday." The words came out in a breathy gush, and she inhaled deeply to deliver the last line with more poise. "Thank you for the invitation." She turned to move swiftly to the door. "I won't take up any more of your valuable time."

He sat looking at the closed door.

"It would appear to me, my dear Miss Freedman," he said to the empty room, "that you're carrying around an awful lot of baggage that Jesus would gladly relieve you of. Why am I so incredibly scary to you?"

He turned his thoughts to prayer. *Well, God, You put her in my path. You made me notice how lonely she is. You gave me the opportunity to speak to her. I forced myself to make the offer of friendship at Your insistent urging and nothing came of it. The project's up-to-date on my end. Now, I guess I'll just wait 'til You show me the next step.*

Jane pushed her cart to the delicatessen area of the grocery store. As she looked over the precooked dinner items, she wondered why it all looked so unappetizing tonight. Even with the financial security she'd built for herself over the last ten years, she still hoarded pennies like the best of misers. By shopping at this time of night, she could get the items marked half price that an hour earlier the store sold full price to the dinner crowd.

She picked up a rotisserie chicken and some thick baked potato slices. She tossed a marked-down, prepackaged Italian salad into the shopping cart for the last item of her evening meal. It should last her two evening meals, especially since it didn't really appeal to her for one.

"Hello," a little voice said at her elbow. Jane looked down into the vaguely familiar face of a lovely sandy-haired child.

"My name's Caroline. We met at church."

"Oh yes, I remember." Jane smiled. "You have two brothers and a sister."

Caroline's face beamed with pleasure. "You remember. It's been weeks, but you remember. I remember, too. You're Miss Freedman. We pray for you at bedtime."

"Me?"

The curls bobbed as Caroline nodded. "I'm shopping with my dad," she volunteered. "We're going to have a picnic for my birthday."

"That's nice," answered Jane with what she hoped was a sincere smile. What else could she say?

"Daddy said your dog was going to have puppies."

Jane genuinely smiled as she remembered the squirming mass of puppies in the box beside her bed.

"Yes, Suggums had five puppies and they are all healthy."

"Can I come see them? I like dogs." She turned up a smiling face dusted with freckles.

"Well, we'll have to ask your father. . . ." She spoke to a departing figure. Caroline raced off to find her dad. Within minutes, Greg Boskell came pushing a cart before him, following his daughter to the lady with the puppies.

"Hello, Jane," he said easily as if their last meeting had not been strained. "Caroline tells me you've invited her over to see the puppies."

"Yes." Jane smiled inanely and hoped she didn't look like an idiot. She couldn't say the child had invited herself. Why did she always feel socially inept in encounters with this man and his children? If anything, that by itself proved her original resolve to keep the relationship strictly professional had been correct. "They're four weeks old now."

"Is tonight convenient? I take it you live near here."

Tonight's not convenient. That's what she needed to say. A simple refusal.

"Yes, just a few blocks over, next to the park."

"Amber Park?"

Caroline jumped up and down. "Please, Daddy, please."

"Wait and see if Miss Freedman already has plans."

Jane looked down into the eager face accentuated by large hopeful eyes trained upon her and could not issue the put-off she'd planned.

"Of course, it's all right," she said. Finally a smile of genuine pleasure warmed her features.

"Are you almost finished shopping or just beginning?" Greg looked at the few measly items in her basket. Groceries and sundries filled his cart to the brim with things packed underneath as well.

"Just two more items," she answered.

"Well, we'll go check out and meet you in the parking lot."

She nodded and turned to head toward the dairy case.

How did I get into this one? I was looking forward to going home and relaxing. Oh well, Suggums always enjoys showing off her brood.

four

"Thanks for carrying my bag. You can put it on the table."

Jane flipped on the light and illuminated the kitchen in all its pristine glory. Not one chair was out of place around the table. A place setting was ready for her dinner. The notepad by the phone was squared off to the corner of the table in perfect symmetry. No dishes sat waiting to be placed in the dishwasher. The room was immaculate.

Suggums jumped up to greet her and Jane introduced Caroline to the mama dog.

"She's adorable," cooed the eight year old, getting down on her knees to be fully greeted by the enthusiastic dog.

"Come this way." Jane led them through the impeccable dining room, the unsullied living room, and the flawless hall to her perfect bedroom. The puppies nestled in a box beside the bed. At the sound of voices in the room, they scrabbled at the sides of their box. Wiggling bits of fur danced eagerly for attention.

While Jane and Caroline fussed over the furry bundles, Greg stood back in the doorway surveying the room that should most intimately reveal the personality of the owner. It was sterile. Feminine, coordinated, elegant, but sterile. His eyes made a sweep of the walls and dresser tops. Not one family picture. No photographs of people.

"Daddy, look at this one. She likes me."

Greg dutifully came forward to sit on the edge of the bed and admire a fur ball of white softness splotched with dark spots. Suggums stood proudly by, as if knowing that the humans admired her offspring.

"Doesn't she mind Caroline holding her pups?" asked Greg.

"No, she eats up all the attention," Jane answered. She

smiled at Caroline. "Besides, she knows Caroline is a trust-worthy admirer."

Jane told her little visitor stories about the first litter of puppies.

"Where are they now?"

"They have nice homes back in Maryland. That's where I used to live."

"You gave them away?"

"Well, actually, I sold them."

"If I had puppies, I wouldn't give even one away."

Jane grinned. "It's hard, I admit. But even Suggums gets tired of them after eight weeks, and it wouldn't be fair to those people who really want a dog if I were to be stingy and keep them all to myself."

"Well, we've got to go and put our groceries away." Greg thanked Jane for the visit and pried his daughter away from the dogs.

"May I come back to see them again?"

"Naturally," said Jane. She'd found it pleasant to share her enthusiasm for the little furry family with a like-minded fan.

❧

The doorbell rang and Jane shifted the swathes of material from her lap to the sofa and set her notebook on the coffee table. The UPS man had already delivered once today, and she wondered what it could be. Caroline's best charming smile surprised her when she opened the door. The young visitor stood with her backpack slung over her shoulder.

"Can I help with the puppies?"

"Shouldn't you go home after school? Won't they miss you?"

"No, I told Aunt Kate I was going to stop here. It's right on the way home. I even wrote her a note and left it in her studio in case she forgets. Sometimes she forgets what you tell her."

"Well, I don't know what you mean by helping me. There really isn't much to do."

"I could change the paper in the box and take them out on the patio to play for a little while."

Jane didn't have the heart to say no to such heartfelt eagerness. "Okay." Jane opened the door wider.

Caroline skipped in and dropped her bags and her coat on the entryway floor. Dashing down the hall she called out, "Hi, Suggums, I've come to play."

Jane picked up the dropped items and placed them on the bench, carefully folding the jacket, and then followed her little visitor.

Suggums wagged her tail and stood alertly by the box watching as Caroline picked up one puppy and then another, giving each a chatty little bit of information about her day at school. Jane sat down on the bed to observe.

After each had been greeted, Caroline turned to Jane.

"What are their names?"

"They don't have official names," she explained. "The new owners will name them."

"They have to have 'meantime' names then," announced Caroline.

"I call that one Scooter. He was the first to push himself all over the box."

"Scooter." Caroline smiled and picked up the named puppy. "Your name is Scooter. You are soooo sweet." She gently hugged it, rubbing the soft fuzzy puppy fur against her cheek. She carefully lowered it back into the box. A cream-colored pup with black markings on its tail and ears whimpered and she scooped it up. "What do you call this one?"

"Burnt Toast."

"Burnt Toast!" Caroline laughed. "That's no name for a beautiful little doggy," she cooed to the puppy, then sat thinking. "How about Cinnamon?"

Jane nodded. "Cinnamon is much better."

"And this one?" She pointed to one of the little black ones.

"I call that one One or Two."

Caroline laughed again. Her laughter bubbled out of her so readily, it made Jane laugh, too.

"Why?"

"Because," said Jane, sounding very reasonable, "the two little black ones are so alike, I call them Black Thing One and Black Thing Two."

"Kind of like *The Cat in the Hat*," exclaimed Caroline, delighted with the idea.

"Exactly. And, since I have to look very closely to see which is which, I usually just say One or Two for either of them."

Caroline laughed again and then she sobered. "But what are you going to do when you sell them? You'll have to know which one is which."

"Well, Black Thing One is a boy and Black Thing Two is a girl."

"Oh, I see." Caroline picked up the last puppy, a white one with tortoiseshell splotches. "Who is this?"

"Sometimes I call her Patches, and sometimes Bully because she pushes everyone out of the way when she wants her mama's milk, and sometimes Rachel. I guess I haven't decided on a name."

"Can I name her?"

"Yes," said Jane.

"I'll have to think about it." She sat gently rubbing the puppy for a very long time. "I'm going to name her Princess Happily Ever After."

"That's a pretty name. Are we to call her Princess?"

"Yes," Caroline sighed. "Can I tell you a secret?"

"Maybe you shouldn't if you really want to keep it a secret."

"Would you tell?" asked Caroline with big eyes.

"No," admitted Jane, "but sometimes the best secrets are the ones you keep the closest to your heart."

She thought about that, then shook her head. "No, I want to tell you."

"Okay."

"This is a special puppy, because I've made a wish upon her."

"I don't think I've ever heard of making a wish upon a puppy."

"It's like making a wish upon a star. You can make a wish upon anything you like. If you really like dolphins, or rainbows, or hummingbirds, you can wish upon any of them."

"I didn't know that."

Caroline shrugged. "It doesn't really matter, because all of it is not really wishing. Wishing doesn't work. It really is talking with God. God hears everything you think and say, especially wishes. God is the only one who can make wishes come true. My dad said so."

"Yes, I think that's right. So are you praying when you make a wish?"

"Not exactly." Caroline's face was serious, her brows pulled down in thought. "Prayer is serious. It's just that when you make a wish, God knows, and because He's the giver of all good things, if the wish comes true it's because He did it. It's kind of like a game you play. He knows the rules and so do you, so it's not really a bad thing as long as you don't get mixed up thinking it's luck or something dumb like that. It's kind of like playing Santa Claus is real with your parents."

"I think I see. Nobody has explained it like that to me before."

"My dad and I worked it out one night. He sometimes comes in and talks to me before I go to sleep. We have great philosophical discussions."

"That's what he calls them?"

"Uh-huh." She nodded.

"So what wish did you make on Princess Happily Ever After?"

"That's the part of the secret I'm not going to tell you."

Jane stuck out her lip in a mock pout and Caroline laughed.

"I promise to tell you if it comes true."

five

"Why don't you come to church anymore?" asked Caroline on Saturday. She was very efficiently rolling up the soiled newspapers to stuff in the plastic garbage bag Jane had ready. During the week, she'd learned just the way Jane liked it done, causing the least amount of mess.

"What makes you think I don't go to church?" asked Jane.

"Well, we only saw you one time," explained Caroline.

Jane held the bag open while Caroline stuffed it, then they both proceeded to lay out the new paper and the old bath towels Jane insisted made the best bed for the puppies.

"There are other churches."

"None as nice as ours," proclaimed Caroline.

"I was just visiting, Caroline," Jane explained. "When you move to a new town, you visit different churches until you find the one you like the best."

"Didn't you like ours the best?"

Jane scowled as she concentrated on smoothing out the towel. Jane *had* liked that church the best and therein lay the problem. The preaching was sound and practical. The music added to the worship. Friendly people had greeted her. When she looked through the bulletin, she saw that the congregation participated in service projects that interested her. But she didn't want to run into the Boskell family every Sunday.

"How was your picnic?" Jane asked to change the subject.

"Great! I'm nine now. Grandma came and she gave me a Walkman."

"CD or tape?" asked Jane.

"Tape."

"What kind of music do you like?"

They talked for awhile about different groups and singers.

Then they transferred the puppies out to the patio and watched as they explored the yard. Jane and Caroline laughed as the puppies tottered on their stubby legs.

The doorbell rang and Suggums dashed into the house to bark at the front door.

❧

"Hello, they tell me at home that my daughter's here." Greg Boskell smiled. He wore blue jeans and a T-shirt that said, "Colorado is great, but don't trust anyone under 14,000 feet." Jane smiled as she read the saying and opened the door wider.

"We're out in the backyard. Join us."

As they walked through the house, Greg again looked at the pristine condition of each of the rooms. He shook his head in amazement, mentally contrasting it to the hodgepodge of junk collected by four kids, an artist sister-in-law, and his own less than tidy self.

"Daddy!" Caroline shouted, jumping up to run into his arms. He lifted her up and gave her a big hug and kiss in greeting.

She began to squirm. "I want you to meet Princess." He let her down and she ran across to the bushes to crawl under and capture the adventuring puppy.

"I've heard a lot about Princess this week," Greg confided to Jane. "I think I'm supposed to fall in love with her and promise she can come home when she's old enough. Has anyone else spoken for her?"

"No," said Jane. "And Caroline is definitely responsible enough for a pet. She's been here every afternoon after school and really helps me."

"I hope she hasn't been a bother."

"Oh no," assured Jane. "I have actually enjoyed her company."

"You sound surprised."

"Well, I don't have any experience with children."

"No brothers, sisters, nieces or nephews?" asked Greg.

"Six big brothers and sisters, lots of nieces and nephews,

tons of cousins of all ages, but, as I said before, I'm the white sheep of the family." Jane sighed. She changed the subject. "The puppy is not taken."

"How much are they?"

"Two hundred fifty. They come with papers."

Greg whistled. "They should have a little more meat on them for that price."

"You were going to eat her? I don't think I'll sell." She smiled at him.

"No, just an expression. We only eat hot dogs. I'll have to think about that price though. I'm more into rescuing dogs from the pound."

Caroline came with Princess cradled in her arms. Greg crouched down to examine the beauty, offering all the appropriate praise for what he called a fur gold mine.

"Why do you call her a gold mine, Daddy?"

"Did Miss Freedman tell you how much they cost?" She shook her head negatively. "Two hundred and fifty bucks."

Caroline looked with big eyes at Jane, and her expression changed to one of resigned disappointment. She put her cheek down on the back of the little body in her arms and closed her eyes. When she put her down a moment later, her face had lost the sorrow.

"Daddy," she demanded, "ask Miss Freedman to come to our church again. She's been visiting. She's just got to try our church again."

Greg turned to the lady beside him. "Miss Freedman," he spoke formally, "I would like to issue you an invitation to come to our church again." He smiled with his best boyish charm and then continued in exactly the same inflection as his daughter. "You've just got to try our church again."

"With such a charming invitation," giggled Jane, "how could I refuse?"

Caroline rewarded her father with a beaming smile.

"Did you attend a Sunday school class last time?" asked Greg.

"No," answered Jane.

"Meet me in the forest at ten to ten, and I'll take you to the one I attend. We're studying the book of James."

"Oh no!" exclaimed Jane in mock horror. "I'll have to guard my unruly tongue."

Greg smiled in appreciation of her humor, but asked sincerely, "Will you come?"

She nodded, the old tenseness stealing through her. Only a moment ago, she had enjoyed the easy camaraderie, and now she felt ill at ease. He'd bridged her outer wall of defense again. That carefully constructed protective wall had not sprung up automatically as it should have.

With this man and his family she had determined to be even more cautious than usual. Not that she was antisocial, she just preferred her life uncomplicated by significant others. She told herself that God was her significant other, and if that wasn't enough to satisfy her soul then she just needed to deepen that relationship.

Jane looked askance at the two Boskells deep in discussion as they crouched over a puppy and rubbed the little upturned belly. Maybe it had been Caroline's daily visits that had breached her wall of solitude. Maybe this father and daughter were a team in cahoots to draw her into the mad machinations of a vibrant Christian family. Maybe they just wanted to rock her boat.

Mentally, she grimaced at her own outlandish thinking. She wanted to take it all lightly, to treat it with humor and thus de-emphasize the significance of their presence in her house.

Well, she thought as she watched Greg and his daughter, *if I can't put a spoke in their wheels, hide behind my walls of isolation, or throw up formidable barriers around my life, I can probably trust Miss Amy to come to my rescue and toss me out the door. Have I just mixed a metaphor? I never have been much good at English. Oh dear, my mind is babbling.*

She smiled what she hoped was a serene smile at her guests and did her best to get them out the front door as quickly as possible. She even agreed to try their church again complete with Sunday school. In order to convince herself that she still maintained some control over the situation, she insisted she had plans for the next day but would join them the following week.

🙦

A pleasant group formed in the Sunday school room. Accustomed to a warm fellowship, these people readily included Jane. A man whose "day job" was as a college professor led a challenging discussion with distinctive expertise. Naturally, Jane sat with Greg during the worship service, and his boys invited her for a quick trip through the drive-thru and hamburgers in the park. The Boskell family dressed more casually today for church and Jane figured this was a planned expedition. Still, *she* hadn't planned on any such thing.

"Honestly, I appreciate the invitation, but I must get back to see to the puppies."

Caroline overheard her excuse.

"Oh, Miss Freedman, can we please take my brothers to see the puppies?"

Jane smiled at her eager helper. She'd grown fond of her and toward the end of the second week managed to get all her work done early so that she could spend some time with Caroline when she arrived after school.

"Sure," she answered cheerfully. "I'll take my car home, and you bring your family after your hamburger picnic in the park."

Amy joined the group under the potted plants at that moment.

"Dad," she said hastily, "Mariann asked if I could go over to her house this afternoon."

"Weren't you over there yesterday?" Greg asked.

"No, I mean, yes, but I was visiting Cameron, and she went over to Mariann's so I went with her."

Greg wore a scowl as if the proposition did not please him. He turned to Jane.

"I don't think I introduced my eldest daughter when you last visited our church."

Jane caught the mulish look that flashed across the girl's face before she managed a neutral expression.

"Miss Freedman, may I introduce my daughter, Amy. Amy, this is Miss Jane Freedman."

"I'm pleased to meet you, Amy," Jane said in just the same tone she had used when meeting more than a dozen other members of the church that morning.

"Hello," said Amy curtly, and turned back to her dad. "Dad, I have to know. I left my homework assignment over there, and if I go now, you won't have to take me over to fetch it later."

"Amy, I had hoped to see something of you myself this afternoon," explained her father.

"Dad, I'm really being rude keeping the Petersons waiting."

"All right, but reserve some of your precious time for your old man tonight. I feel like I haven't visited with you since last week."

Amy darted off without even a good-bye, and Jane felt Greg's embarrassment over her bad manners.

"I'm sorry," he said, "she usually isn't so. . ."

"She was just eager to be off with her friends." Jane provided an excuse.

Greg nodded his head, but she could see unusual lines of concern on his forehead. The other children swamped him with suggestions as to which local fast-food restaurant was going to get their business.

"Why don't you tell us what you want and we'll pick it up?" he suggested to Jane. "You can run home to the puppies and then join us."

"No, that's too much bother."

"Please," begged Caroline. She took her new friend's hand and looked up with beseeching eyes.

Jane studied the earnest face with affection. This little girl successfully wrapped Jane around her finger. Jane would soon have to put an end to it. But maybe not today.

six

When Jane walked into her house twenty minutes later, she found the puppies had scrambled over the edge of the cardboard box. Jane cleaned up the little puddles and other "accidents" before she changed her clothes. They had also attacked a box of tissue and scattered little torn bits all over her bedroom. Then they'd curled up on some large scatter pillows artfully piled in the corner of her living room. Only one small piece of the fringe was chewed beyond repair.

Jane cleaned the spots on the rug, picked up the tissue, and emptied her laundry basket. She put an old towel in the laundry basket, put a leash on Suggums, and loaded the pups into the basket to carry to the park.

"I'm not leaving you guys alone again until I rig up a better box," she scolded mildly and carried them out the front door to walk down the street and across to Amber Park.

She arrived just as Greg pulled up in his minivan with the children. Caroline came racing across to greet her.

"You brought them," she squealed with glee. "Jake, Tom, come see!" She raced back to the parked car, but her brothers met her halfway, and she turned to run back, calling over her shoulder, "Daddy, Miss Freedman brought the puppies."

Jane laughed at her enthusiasm. Every person in the neighborhood must know the puppies were at the park. A crowd of children, several ladies, and a couple of men all wanted to see her puppies.

The little girls and older women cooed over the fur balls. One man commented that they were cute little rascals but didn't they grow up to be dust mops? Jane didn't take offense and answered questions about the breed and how much they cost. One lady took her phone number. Finally, the people drifted away.

ã

"I think our hamburgers are getting cold," Greg said. He'd stood back and admired the way Jane handled the situation. For someone who claimed no expertise with children, she had handled the multitude of kids with aplomb.

They spread out a blanket, as all the picnic tables were already claimed, and sat down to devour his offering. The boys wanted to feed the puppies, but Caroline informed them they only drank Suggums' milk so far.

"Then can we give Suggums some French fries?"

"No," answered Jane kindly. "Any form of potatoes is very hard on a dog's digestive system. You can give her your last bite of hamburger as long as it is a very tiny bite."

So Suggums got three little bites of hamburger and bun before the children ran off to explore the elaborate jungle gym. It was shaped like two rocket ships with two suspension bridges crossing at different points and a curling chute slide from the top of one rocket spiraling around the outside to the ground. A sphere with giant holes also connected to the apparatus. It represented some kind of planet, or maybe the moon.

The puppies played for awhile on the blanket, with Greg and Jane retrieving them each time they ventured beyond the edge. Soon they sought out their mother, got a drink, then snuggled down for a nap.

"So why did you decide to bring the puppies to the park?" asked Greg. He laid on his side, propped up on an elbow, watching this intriguingly different woman. Until today, he had thought of her as only a cold fish who needed some local friends. Today she wore a modishly scruffy outfit—khaki slacks, and a dark blue sweatshirt with the collar of a white shirt neatly showing at the neck. He gladly observed that her white tennis shoes were less than white and thought she might not be living with Mr. Clean on the sly after all.

Jane grinned at him and answered, "The beasties had escaped their confines and demolished three rooms before I arrived home from church."

She laughed, which Greg found incongruous considering what she had just said. Greg was surprised at how calmly Jane took the damage to her beautiful things. From the appearance of the whole house, he had assumed that Jane was a neat freak, and that more than anything had concerned him when Caroline related where she was spending her afternoons. He couldn't see this coolly professional woman allowing his rambunctious daughter to tear up her peace.

Caroline came across as a shy one until she accepted a new friend. Then she was as gregarious and as boisterous as the boys. He'd waited for the news that Miss Freedman was going to be too busy for any more visits, but instead Caroline assured him that her new friend invited his little girl back. Caroline sang Jane's praises anytime she wasn't subtly trying to convince him of a certain puppy's fine qualities.

He adjusted his opinion of her yet again as he enjoyed the warmth of her unaffected smile. Greg had merely meant to fill the silence with a topic, any topic. He'd chosen the dogs because he'd noted that they brought out the soft side of her.

He watched Jane carefully, noting the wind ruffling her hair, the way her eyes crinkled at the corners when she smiled, the gentleness with which she stroked a sleeping pup with one well-manicured finger. Intrigued, he almost forgot to listen to what she was saying.

"Actually," she continued, "they were resting from their rampage on my best living room cushions." She lightheartedly described the havoc they had created.

"Didn't that make you angry?" he asked bluntly.

"Angry?" She seemed puzzled. "Oh, because of the mess? Well, puppies make a mess, don't they? I'll have to devise a better pen though. In Maryland, for the last litter, I had a baby's playpen I had acquired at a garage sale."

"They chewed the fringe on your pillows, and you don't care?"

Jane lifted puzzled eyebrows. *Surely,* she thought, *this man should be used to youngsters inadvertently destroying property.*

"Are you some kind of a neat freak?" she asked.

An odd grimace came over his face and he screwed his eyes shut. Then, he leaned back on the blanket staring into the sky with a gentle chortle escaping him. To Jane it sounded like some kind of a strangled groan. He began to shake a little harder with the laughter that sprang up within, once more screwed his eyes shut, and tried to confine it, which made him turn red and make choking, snorting noises.

Jane put a hand on his shoulder.

"Greg," she said urgently, "are you all right?"

He opened his eyes and looked up at her concerned face. It was too much. His laughter came out in a blast, and he rolled away, allowing himself room to really enjoy the humor.

Finally, he began to get some control over his outburst and wiped the tears from his eyes with the sleeve of his jacket. The boys came charging back and tackled their dad.

"We saw you laughing from the top of the rocket, Daddy," said Jake. "Tell us what's funny."

"Miss Freedman thought I might be a neat freak," he explained between gasps. Jake looked puzzled, but Tom went off in a peal of laughter not unlike his father's. When Greg saw his younger son's confusion, he tried to explain. "It means that Daddy puts things away."

Light dawned on the little face and he grinned at Jane. "You'll have to come see our house. We have paths between the junk piles so you can get from room to room. Grandma won't come anymore and two maids quit."

Greg hung his head and tried to look ashamed, but there was still a glimmer of humor in his eyes.

"I thought your sister-in-law took care of your house."

Greg shook his head. "Oh no, she's as bad as the rest of us. She and my wife had a studio on the third floor in our house. After Kathy died, Kate continued to work at the house, and that works out fine. She's the on-site adult if the kids need anything. If anyone is the housekeeper, it's Amy. She's always been the reliable one."

The brothers laid down and the puppies proceeded to climb all over them, chewing on their hair and clothing. Caroline came back to join in the fun, and when the puppies tired of the play, the children deserted them.

Jane had sat back on her heels during Greg's outburst, wondering what in the world had made him laugh like a hyena. She went back over their conversation. He didn't seem to see the humor in the puppies' little demolition derby, but was more concerned over the mess.

Perhaps he was just seeing the funny side that I saw more easily, she thought. *Really, that display was a little extreme. Well, he's a man who deals with figures and wood and angles and whatnot. Perhaps his sense of humor is a trifle retarded.*

Greg had watched the antics of his children and the puppies with enjoyment, but Jane felt he was really concentrating on something else. When the children left, he didn't try to restart their conversation, and she sat contentedly watching the activities in the park, occasionally retrieving a straying pup.

"It was unusual for Amy to abruptly change plans today," he finally said, almost to himself. Jane made no comment. "She'd planned to come with us. She's usually very polite in her conversations with adults, and today she ignored you to the point of rudeness."

"I wasn't offended," said Jane.

"I am." Greg grimaced. "Amy's almost the perfect child. As the oldest, she's always been more than a good example for the others, and really, it must have been something my wife trained into her. It certainly didn't come from me." He paused in reflection.

"Kathy was a marvelous person. She was fun and artistic like her sister and kind of a flake at times, but what a wonderful mother!" Greg was silent for awhile. "You know, I don't talk about her much. I hope you don't mind."

Jane shook her head but realized he wasn't looking at her, so she verbalized, "No, of course not."

"Kate had taken a load of their work to a gallery, so Kathy was alone with the children. She had a heart attack. Out of the blue. Nobody suspected there was any problem. Amy called 911, and then hung up, even though they told her to stay on the line. She just told them she had to locate her dad. She systematically went through my log book and found me. I didn't even know how serious it was. She sounded so calm I thought it must have been just a minor emergency, but since she explained Kate had gone to the gallery—she even knew which one—and Mom couldn't come to the phone, I told her I'd be right there.

"The ambulance was in the driveway when I arrived, and they were loading my wife in the back. The children were standing beside a neighbor woman. I said something to them—but I can't tell you what—and climbed in the back of the ambulance with Kathy.

"The neighbor, Mrs. Kranz, must have thought Kate was in the house, because she went home. Or maybe she was just so shocked, she didn't think at all. She was ancient at the time. She's died since then. I assumed she would stay with the kids. I guess I wasn't thinking either.

"But Amy gathered up the little ones. She was nine, Jake was just walking, Tom was almost three, Caroline was five. She took them inside, fed them their lunch, and put them down for a nap. She washed up the blood on the studio floor where Kathy's head had hit something and bled all over the place. She cleaned up the debris the paramedics had left behind. She started a load of laundry because of all the bloody rags from her cleanup job. She did it all without any panic. I don't think she realized that Kathy would not be coming back. I know I certainly didn't believe it was happening."

He paused and Jane watched his face. She was relieved to see that he must have worked through his grief, because this recital was not an emotional thing. He was worried about something, and she felt that all of this was just a precursor to the real problem.

"Kathy never regained consciousness. I just thought things at home were being taken care of. And they were. The children got up from their naps. Amy changed diapers, put a video in, and kept them out of trouble. When it got dark, she called Grandma Standish, but I had called her earlier, and she'd come to the hospital. She called the gallery, but Kate had made the delivery and was on the way home. It was clear across town and what with one thing and another, Kate just went to her own home afterward. Amy had left her a message on the answering machine, telling her what hospital her sister was in. Kate showed up just as they told us that Kathy had died."

He was silent again, and Jane wondered if she should say something. She bit her lower lip. She thought of the grief-stricken family, suddenly deprived of someone who, for apparently no reason, had died. Tears welled up in her own eyes, and she prayed that she wouldn't embarrass Greg by bursting out with unwanted tears. He was obviously trying to work something out. He talked aloud and to her, but he didn't seem to need her to enter into the conversation. In fact, it would probably be distracting.

"I didn't get home until late. I'd been gone over ten hours. Amy'd put dinner on the table, bathed the little ones, and put them down for the night. She was asleep in the big rocker in the living room. That was when I realized she had gone through all of that alone. None of us thought. We all assumed. Nobody said, 'Who's with the kids?'

"I picked her up and sat down in the chair and just held her, rocking her. She didn't wake up until hours later, when I too had gone to sleep. She woke me up, and told me I had to go to bed. I think she took me by the hand and led me up the stairs. I told her her mother had died, and she said, 'I know, Daddy. We'll talk about it in the morning.'

"I was numb, and I followed her directions to get in bed. She left and I cried myself to sleep. It's horrible lying in a bed alone, knowing the one who's supposed to be there will never be there again."

Jane nodded, but he didn't see.

"The visitors, the cards, the flowers, the funeral, more visitors, more flowers, more cards. It was weeks and weeks before I began to function with any sense of normalcy, and when I did, I realized how mature Amy had been through it all. Everyone praised her for her actions during the crisis. I don't remember her being anything but a normal little girl before. Afterward, she was capable, extremely capable, and responsible. The experience changed her, not necessarily in a bad way, but I didn't exactly like it. I had to work at not being irritated at her for being so mature. I wanted everything to be the same as it was before that awful day."

A long stretch of silence followed. Jane didn't know what to say. Should she offer words of comfort? She didn't know what they might be. Was there a bit of wisdom that would help this troubled father? She'd never considered herself particularly wise. She prayed. *Lord, I don't know what all this means, but I see some hurting people here and I know You want to help. If I need to say something, please put the words in my mouth.* She remembered the way the conversation had begun.

"And now," said Jane, "you're wondering about this unusual behavior today?"

Greg looked up at her and smiled, nodding.

"She's only thirteen," he said. "She did something unexpected. She was rude to an adult."

Jane looked puzzled.

"That's typical of a teenager," he continued. "Amy's not been typical for her age in over four years."

"It's a good sign?" asked Jane.

"Maybe," said Amy's dad.

seven

The telephone rang and Jane picked it up.

"Hi! You still awake?" Greg's cheerful voice came over the line.

"Yes," said Jane, disturbed that he'd call after they'd spent the entire afternoon together. They'd parted about five o'clock when he loaded up his children in the minivan while she'd loaded up her puppies in the basket.

"I found our old playpen in the attic," Greg explained. "I'll bring it over."

"Tonight?"

"Sure, it's only a couple of blocks." He hesitated. "Have you already rigged something up?"

Jane thought of the puppies currently residing in her bathtub. "They're sleeping in my bathroom," she said. After only a moment's deliberation, she sighed. "Bring it on over."

She hadn't even offered a token resistance to the man's charm this time. It was ten o'clock and she was inviting him into her home again.

Something is wrong with this picture. Well, I need the playpen, but I don't need to be friendly about it. I'll be businesslike and civil, but not enthusiastic about this late-night visit.

Jane caught a glimpse of herself in the mirror and dashed to her room to remove the comfy robe. She kicked her fluffy slippers into the closet and closed the door. She opened the hamper lid and dragged out her earlier outfit. The doorbell rang as she dragged a brush through her short curls. This man disturbed her normal routine, a routine that she had made an effort to establish and protect. He was *not* welcome. So why did a smile pop up on her face when she opened the door?

Greg brought the playpen right into the bedroom and helped her set it up and then wash it down.

"It's been up in the attic for years," he explained the dust and dirt.

"You realize that after the pups get through with it, it will be in no shape for babies."

"Well, I'm obviously not going to need it again," chuckled Greg.

Jane smiled.

This guy is getting to me, she begrudgingly admitted to herself. *He has a nice easy manner. He's busy with his career and family, and yet he took the time to find this old playpen for the pups. Maybe I shouldn't be treating him like the carrier of some dread disease.*

"Are your kids all tucked in bed?" she asked as they laid out papers and old towels in the bottom of the playpen.

"Yes, there's nothing like a day in the park to pave the way for an easy bedtime. It's already the first of October, and there won't be many more days pleasant enough to spend that much time out-of-doors."

She wondered if he'd had his time with Amy that he had mentioned during the conversation at church, but decided it was not her business. She asked a general topic question instead.

"Do you dread the winter months?"

"Live in Colorado and dread winter? Not likely."

"Do you ski?"

"I did when I was young," admitted Greg. "I saw a sign once that said it was the only sport that cost you an arm and a leg to break an arm and a leg. After college, I was just too interested in other things. Are you going to try it?"

Jane shook her head with a big grin on her face. "Not me."

They laughed together. Greg looked at her with that crooked grin.

Just friends, thought Jane, *it's nice to just be friends.*

"The pups are in my bathtub." She rose to her feet and he followed her to transfer them to their new jailhouse.

"Amy lied to me," Greg said as he put the last pup in.

"What?" asked Jane, startled by the abrupt introduction to a new subject, a personal one at that.

"She lied to me," he repeated.

Jane didn't ask any questions. This was *not* her business.

"She told me she left her homework over at a friend's and instead, it was at home on the hallway table."

"She was mistaken," offered Jane.

Greg shook his head sadly. "I don't think so."

"More typical teen behavior?"

Greg looked up at her and grinned sheepishly.

"The parent worries when his child does not display typical behavior and then worries when she does." He looked completely befuddled. "It's just that I don't believe our society's definition of normal teenage behavior is what our Almighty God intended."

"You know, Greg," Jane said softly, "I'm not really the person to talk to about this. I have no experience. Maybe the pastor, or if the church has a youth pastor, he could help. Or, maybe even a professional counselor."

"Yeah," said Greg, "I'm sorry. I guess it's on my mind a lot."

"I don't mind. It's just that I don't see how I'd be much help. Maybe your parents, or your sister-in-law, or your wife's parents?"

"They all think Amy's fine." Greg shook his head and stuck his hands in the pockets of his sweater jacket. "I think she's fine, too. I tell her often enough how proud I am of her." Greg shrugged. "I'd better go. See you soon."

"Sure." She nodded and showed him to the front door.

When she went to bed, her thoughts kept returning to the man who had offered her friendship even after being rudely rebuffed for weeks on end. He really was a nice man, and she was sorry he was having family troubles, but she was right in not getting involved.

What do I know about families? I wasn't even raised in one like most people.

She thought about her situation growing up. Her youngest older sibling had been in high school when she was born. She was a "surprise baby," born to her mother after her mother was a grandmother through an older child. She had six older brothers and sisters, none of whom she knew very well. They had all been grown and gone by the time she was three or four and counting the people around the house.

Her father was a gruff man, getting more cantankerous by the year. Her mother was a whiny person, given to taking to her bed with a bottle of whatever she could scrounge up. Her drinking became more of problem as Jane grew older. She remembered when she was about Caroline's age, she began coming home from school and fixing dinner because her mother had spent the day with her drinking friends. Sometimes her mother would come home, sometimes she would not. It got to be more not. Then, in junior high, she learned how her mother was earning the money to buy her booze. A boy had explained how he'd paid ten dollars to her mother, but would be glad to give her twenty for the same service. Jane went home, packed a bag, and left.

She went down the street to Mrs. Grehurst, the lady who had a Bible club in her house every Thursday afternoon. A teacher would come and play some games, teach them songs, and tell a Bible story. Then there were snacks, better than anything Jane ever got at home. And then there was the missionary story. Jane loved the exciting missionary story, and she loved Mrs. Grehurst who lived in the house, a house that felt like a real home. She accepted Christ to make Mrs. Grehurst happy. Mrs. Grehurst welcomed her into her home long after the kids her age had found something else to do on Thursday afternoons. She even let Jane teach the memory verse sometimes.

Jane's initial decision based on pleasing Mrs. Grehurst sometime along the way became a decision for herself alone. Jane realized it made her happy. She had God to talk to in the night when her mother and father were yelling and throwing things. She pretended in the morning when she got up by her-self, fixed her own breakfast, and got ready for school, that her Heavenly Father chatted to her, right beside her, every minute, and then said good-bye with a big hug and a kiss as she went out the door. Of course, that had been when she was younger. By the time she packed her bag, her relationship had gone from fantasy to reality. Her faith had grown. She knew that Jesus would never leave her. The trust and love that were missing in her parents was strong in her Heavenly Father.

It was a disappointment that Mrs. Grehurst couldn't keep her. It was shattering when the kind lady explained that she and her husband were moving away. But that caused Jane to hold on more tightly to the One who wouldn't disappoint her or be bound by earthly encumbrances such as moving to a retirement home. Jane prayed with Mrs. Grehurst. Mrs. Grehurst called the authorities.

Jane ended up at her sister's house, and then at another sis-ter's house, and then another, and another, and then her brother's house. The last brother wouldn't even offer to take her for one night.

That's when the loudest of her long memory of fights broke loose. That's when she got on the bus and went downtown to her mother's youngest sister. She left them fighting. She didn't even remember who was there to do the yelling. She just went upstairs, got her suitcase, and left down the back stairs. Her aunt ran a coffee house/bookstore downtown where all sorts of people hung out. Aunt Nelda wouldn't mind one more misfit.

Jane assumed the people back at her sister's house noticed she was gone. She never heard from them until she was grown and stopped by to renew the acquaintanceship. They weren't interested, especially when they heard she was an active mem-ber of a church that worked with inner-city "riffraff."

"You were picked out of the gutter by those holier-than-thou hypocrites?"

"No, I wasn't picked out of any gutter. I just went to church there one Sunday. It was the closest one, and I could walk on

Sundays and Wednesday nights."

"One of those goody-goodies who go to church every time the doors are open? That's what you are? You know, I think Dad's right. Mom must have brought you home as a gift from one of her 'friends.' You're sure not like any Freedman I ever knew. We don't mess with God and Jesus and all that church stuff. Dad always said he was suspicious how Mom got pregnant that last time without much help from him."

The implications horrified Jane. It explained a lot though. The lack of love. The cold indifference of her father. Jane stumbled out of there and never went back, never tried to meet with any of the others who were supposed to be her family. She read of her dad's death in the obituaries and went to the funeral. Nobody spoke to her. Maybe they didn't recognize her. She didn't care. She noticed her mother wasn't there and she wondered why. Six years later, she still didn't know.

Aunt Nelda had accepted her help around the shop. Gave her a room. Never yelled at her, and respected her religious choices as long as she didn't interfere with Nelda's choices. The church down the street from her aunt's store had nurtured her in a distant way. They were really more concerned with the people who actually lived on the street. But it was through them that she got jobs, and then help registering for college, and occasionally some money for expenses.

Why am I dwelling on this, Lord? I praise You that You accepted me into Your family. I haven't thought about this in years. I'm not bound by the past when I couldn't be a little girl because there was no one to treat me like a cherished little girl.

The thought gave her reason to pause. *No, Lord, that's not it. Amy has many people who cherish her.* The next words came to her mind as clearly as if spoken to her.

But does she think of herself as a little girl, or has she taken on that mature personality that she adopted in a moment of terror?

What do I know about her, Lord? The list formed in her

mind immediately after her brief prayer. Amy showed remarkable presence of mind in a very emotional crisis. She was praised for it. She continued the performance. Got more praise. They told her she had taken charge and that was good. When she talked to me at Mike's Midtown Burgers she was trying to take control of the situation. There was no "situation," but she didn't realize that.

She didn't want me to come in and change things.

I remember how I did not want things to change. Every time I went to another house, I wanted it to be the last time I was shifted around. I was desperate to just stay in one place. They kept moving me. I wasn't even consulted. I'd come home from school and someone would tell me to go pack my suitcase. I'd see signs it was about to happen again and try to fend it off. I'd be extra good, extra helpful, extra quiet. Nothing I did worked. If I could have been the one in charge. . .

She almost gasped aloud as she realized where this was leading.

I would have given anything to be the one in charge. I wonder if Amy has given up being a child in order to feel like she's in control.

I think Miss Amy Boskell has more gumption than I ever had. But maybe it isn't gumption she needs. Maybe she needs to give up some of that gumption and depend on her dad, and even more importantly, on God.

Oh Lord, this sounds like a lot of psychology and theology and a whole bunch of other things I'm not willing to touch. Maybe I'll get a chance to just mention this to Greg, and he can take her to a professional counselor.

eight

Jane looked up from her novel at the clock on the mantel when the doorbell rang. Eight-thirty. Who would be out on this cold night? Earlier, two groups of children had come by selling candy bars for some fund-raiser at school. Of course, Caroline had already sold her two bars, and her brothers had tagged along for what they must have known would be an easy mark. She now had six of the thick chocolate bars in her freezer. Could she possibly manage to say no this time?

She peeked through the small hole at eye level in her front door and was surprised to see the distorted image of Greg Boskell. His hooded sweatshirt jacket shielded him against the nippy air. He carried a tool chest.

A smile sprang to her lips and she felt a rush of pleasure. Just before she flung open the door, the voice of habit echoed in her ear. *He's a complication. He's a difficulty. He represents entanglement.* This was just the sort of dilemma that she had consciously avoided for years. The smile slipped. With a wary looked on her face, she opened the door.

"What are you doing here?" she asked.

He grinned. "Plumbing service, Ma'am," he answered, ignoring the rather unconventional greeting she'd given him. "Caroline says your hose on the washer is leaking."

"Well, yes, but I was going to call the service company in the morning."

"I'm here now, and Caroline says you do about two loads of old towels a day for the puppies."

Jane looked at his friendly face seeing the willingness to help. Caroline had sent him.

"I'm being awfully rude," she apologized. "Come in."

She let him pass and closed the door tightly against the

night air. He stood in the entryway looking tall and competent and altogether too attractive. Jane heaved a big sigh and leaned back against the door.

"Greg, I appreciate your offer, but I'm accustomed to taking care of myself. It will be inconvenient to wait a few days for the service man, but it isn't impossible." She looked at the frown that had darkened his features and felt she had better continue on to establish some ground rules. She did not want to get involved with this man and his family. Amy's problems needed professional help. She had no right to advise him or offer her opinions. Amy was his business, not hers. She didn't want to be involved. If he kept intruding on her life, and if she continued to respond to the sight of him with this stupid bubbly joy, it was going to get out of hand.

"I don't need someone stepping in and taking care of things. I really am all right. I'm not lonely for family and friends left in Maryland. I make enough money to hire people to fix things. You're a busy man and it makes me feel uncomfortable that I'm intruding on your time."

He stood silently watching her for a moment. She wondered what he was thinking. His face sure didn't give anything away. Finally, his eyebrows rose an inch and that charming grin brightened his face.

"*Yo comprendo, señorita,*" he said.

"What?"

"I understand," he translated. "However, I'm here, and if you'll fix me a cup of coffee, I'll look at the washer and feel good about my knight-errant act in spite of the fact that my damsel in distress slays her own dragons. Caroline says you are her special friend and she expects me to take care of you."

Doubt still hovered on Jane's face, and he added in a more serious tone, "I promise to check with you before charging to the rescue next time. It really did not occur to me that this would bother you. It's just something I know how to do. The leaky hose is probably a very minor fix-it job."

Jane looked into his eyes and saw nothing but his usual

friendly expression. A little embarrassed by her niggardly acceptance of his generous help, she smiled awkwardly.

"Thanks," she said. "Thanks for the offer of help, and thanks for not being angry at my reluctance to accept it. The washer is back here."

She led the way to the little laundry room constructed as a remodeling job between her bedroom and the bathroom. Wet towels cluttered the floor and Jane scooped them up, throwing them into an empty laundry basket. She turned and Greg stood directly behind her in the small opening.

He smelled of spice cologne. His chin had a faint day-end stubble. He'd removed his jacket and the muscles of his shoulders stretched the material of his T-shirt.

This is why this is wrong! Her brain screamed at her. *The stupid man is kind to his children, friendly to strangers, intelligent, modestly well-off financially, a practicing Christian, looks good, smells good, and drives me crazy. He probably was an Eagle Scout and still helps little old ladies across the street. I don't want anything to do with him. I don't want him in my house. I don't want him in my life!*

"I'll fix the coffee," she said.

He moved aside and she squeezed past him. *He could have moved over a little more,* she thought. *MEN!*

The little two-cup drip machine finished the coffee just as Greg entered the kitchen. Jane deliberately didn't go back to watch him work. Instead, she stayed in the kitchen, setting out two mugs, the creamer and sugar bowl, spoons, a plate of cookies, and napkins.

Greg walked over to the kitchen sink and washed his hands with soap, getting off the black stain left by the rubber hose. He turned off the faucet and stood with his hands and arms dripping surgeon style as he looked at the delicate floral hand towel folded precisely and hanging by the sink.

"Something wrong?" asked Jane.

"I don't want to mess up the towel."

She tossed him an odd look, tugged the towel off its ring,

and handed it to him.

"That's what it's there for." Her tone implied humor more than sarcasm and Greg grinned as he took it.

She poured the coffee and they sat at the table.

"It's decaf," she explained. "I hope that's okay."

"Um," he said lifting the mug to his lips.

"Have you decided about the puppy?" Jane asked by way of a conversation starter.

"Caroline sure wants her," he answered, taking a cookie.

"Would you like a candy bar?" Jane asked with a grin.

"One for the new playground equipment?" he asked, catching on quickly to that hint in her voice. "No thanks, I have ten of them at home."

Jane laughed, relaxing a little.

"Have you sold all the puppies?"

"Not Princess, but all the others are spoken for," she answered. "I won't let them go home until they're about eight weeks old."

"I thought it was six weeks."

"Lots of people do. It is really better for them to spend the extra two weeks with their mother. Some cities even have ordinances that puppies and kittens can't be sold or given away until they are eight weeks old."

"I never would have thought it mattered," said Greg.

The conversation lagged. Jane searched for something to say.

"I enjoy Caroline's visits, and today the boys stayed for about an hour. She's helped me every afternoon, and I suppose she'll continue to come until the puppies are gone. What would you say if I were to tell her that she has worked a hundred dollars off the price of the puppy? That might make her feel good about herself as well as making her feel like the puppy is really hers and therefore her responsibility."

Greg looked at her in amazement.

"Is that all right?" Jane asked. "I don't really breed Suggums for the profit. I just like having the puppies."

Greg shook himself. "Yes, yes, that's wonderful. It's just

that it was unexpected. I mean, you said that you didn't know a thing about children and yet, you get along with them beautifully, and that is an excellent plan for her to acquire what she wants. Are you sure you're not hiding a degree in child psychology in your background?"

It was Jane's turn to be nonplussed. A lot of things lurked in her background. She didn't exactly keep them hidden but neither did she bring them out and shake them in front of people to see. The phone rang before she had a chance to answer.

She stood up to go pick up the receiver.

"Hello," she answered. "Aunt Nelda?"

Greg picked up the dishes from the table and took them over to the sink. In a moment, he had the few things washed off and put in the drainer. He put the little cream pitcher back in the refrigerator and wiped the few crumbs he'd left into the palm of his hand and brushed them off in the sink. It was then he noticed that Jane was not speaking. He came back to the table and saw her standing in the corner. The telephone had been returned to the cradle, but Jane just stood facing the wall, her arms crossed over her middle as if she were hugging herself. The image projected something very distraught.

"Jane," he said softly. She didn't answer. He took a quick step forward.

"Jane," he spoke from directly behind her and still she seemed not to hear. He touched her shoulder and gently turned her. Her eyes were closed and instinctively, he put an arm across her shoulders pulling her closer.

"Jane, was it bad news?"

"I don't know," she whispered. "I can't decide how I feel."

"What happened?"

"My mother died." Greg's arm tightened around her and her eyes flew open. She pulled away, and he immediately released her.

"It's not what you think. She was a prostitute. I haven't seen her since I was fifteen. I honestly thought she must have died years ago. She was found in an. . .in an. . .in an alley."

Jane stuttered over the last words and now she cried. Greg reached out and took her in his arms again, leaning her head against his shoulder and gently rubbing her back. She cried as if a dam had broken within her. For several minutes, the torrent flowed without control.

"She never was a mother." She managed to sob out the words eventually. "Why should I cry for someone who never loved me?" Greg led her into the living room and urged her to sit down on the sofa. He sat down next to her, holding both her trembling hands in his large steady one.

She wept quietly now that the initial storm had passed. Of her own accord, she leaned against him and settled down against his chest. He let go of her hands to further encircle her in a sheltering embrace.

Greg didn't speak while she cried. His thoughts jumbled with prayer for her grief even though he couldn't understand it.

As the weeping grew softer, he heard her sniffle and he reached across the end table to the box of tissues.

"Here." He offered the whole box. She took a handful and blew her nose, wiped her tears, and blew some more.

"I'm so sorry," she apologized.

Greg shrugged.

"Oh," she lamented, looking at his chest. "I got your shirt all soppy."

He shrugged again.

"You're a great counselor," she reproved him with a tiny smile hovering at the corner of her mouth.

"I haven't a clue as to what to say so I thought I'd go for the strong, silent type."

A tiny laugh escaped her and Jane took in a long breath and let it out slowly.

"Isn't that odd?" she commented. "I would have sworn I had no emotional baggage left over from that source. I quit feeling intensely about my childhood while I was living with my aunt Nelda. She had many strange philosophies and one of the useful ones was the serenity prayer. You know, 'God grant me the serenity to accept the things I can not change.' It was not quoted as a link to Christianity but more as wisdom imparted by the Universal Center of Peace."

Greg lifted his eyebrows in a question.

"Aunt Nelda's into New Age, Old Age, Western, Eastern, Southern, Northern and Mid-Atlantic philosophy."

"Mid-Atlantic?"

"There's a magnetic force centered in some ocean. It might have been Pacific. I really don't remember. She embraced all spiritual thought because they harmonized within her. It was her gift." She quirked an eyebrow at Greg, watching how he would receive evidence of more depravity in her family.

He just smiled, and asked, "How is it you're a Christian?"

"God's grace." She smiled at the simple answer.

"Are you going to return for the funeral?" Greg asked.

"No." She wrapped her arms tight around her midsection. "They already had the funeral. I wasn't invited." Jane's answer unlocked the guard she kept on her past. Out of that simple beginning she ended up telling him a condensed account of her childhood. She began with the happy account of the Friend and Father God who kept her company whenever she was lonely. She included the months of being shuffled from one sibling to another and wound up at her aunt Nelda's where she wasn't loved, but she wasn't berated either.

"Do you mind if I practice my little knowledge of psychology on you?" asked Greg when she'd paused.

She gave him a skeptical look. "I'm not sure I'm up to that."

"You can throw me out if it upsets you, but I honestly only want to help."

"Okay," she said without enthusiasm.

"I think the bout of tears was for your mother. Not the mother whom you haven't seen in years, nor the mother who had deserted you emotionally before that. But for the mother whose life died years before you even knew her. The woman died in such a way that she continued to live, but without hope. She was incapable of giving love and yet remained among the living in a dead existence. It was just that sort of lost individual that Jesus wept for. He didn't weep for those He knew He could reach."

Jane watched his face intently as he spoke.

"Jane," he continued, "it's all right to weep for someone that you wanted to love but were never given the opportunity."

She nodded. "I wanted her to have the chance to change. She was bound by alcoholism. Her life didn't show fruit. That hurt her as well as me. Maybe, in the end, someone reached her with God's love. That would be a miracle, and God is still doing them."

"That's right," agreed Greg.

Jane smiled at him. "You've been awfully good to me tonight." She sighed and leaned back against the cushions. "I went to a neighborhood church while I lived with Aunt Nelda. It was a downtown street ministry. I would fantasize that somehow through them I would run into my mother and offer her God's love. Each scenario I imagined ended the same way. She would accept Christ through my intervention and then she would love me."

"Sounds like a reasonable desire to me."

"Well, I was rather obsessive about it for awhile. Then I decided the desire was more about me than about my mother, and I determined that when that daydream came to mind, I would turn it into a prayer for God to reach her regardless of whom He used to do it." She looked over at the clock. "Good grief, Greg, it's after midnight."

✿

Greg collected his tools and his jacket. When they reached the front door, Jane tried to think of something to say that would let him know how much she appreciated his staying with her. She was embarrassed by the way she'd tried to turn him out when he first arrived.

"Greg," she said softly, "I want to apologize for giving you such a hard time when you came over. It's ironic, isn't it? You were here to fix the leaky faucet, and I turned into the leakiest faucet around."

He grinned and leaned over to kiss her forehead lightly.

"I forgot to tell you there's an extra charge for floods."

He opened the door and waved nonchalantly as he went down the drive to his van.

"You'll get my bill in the mail," he called back.

She smiled and closed the door.

I'm fighting a losing battle, Lord. No one has ever kissed me on the forehead. Are You listening to me at all? I don't want to be dependent on this man. Can't we just go back to You being my sole comfort and guardian?

She went into the kitchen to put things away and noticed for the first time that Greg had cleaned up while she was on the phone. *He didn't have to do that,* she thought. *He does a lot of things he doesn't have to. But, it was nice to have someone here tonight. Thank You, Lord.*

She switched out the lights and went back to her bedroom. The puppies were piled in a corner of the playpen, cozily accepting the warmth of their togetherness. Suggums lifted her head and peered sleepily at her owner. Jane undressed and crawled into bed. Suggums left her babes and jumped up on the bed to curl in the old familiar spot behind Jane's knees.

It was comfortable having her canine friend so close.

"Suggums," Jane said aloud. "I have you for the touchy-feely companionship, and I have the Lord for every other relationship I need. He's my parent, my friend, my confidante, my teacher, my everything. I don't need a man, especially a man with four kids."

She adjusted her pillow and looked over at the lighted dial of her alarm clock. Only fifteen minutes had passed since Greg had walked out her door. It seemed like a long time, yet the time from when he arrived to when he left had sped by.

"No argument," she said sternly into the night to the unconcerned dog. "We don't need him!"

nine

"Put your hands in the air, Ma'am. We're here to arrest you."
Tom's eyes looked at her solemnly from behind the silver pistol aimed at her person. It wiggled around some so Jane wasn't sure exactly where she'd be hit if he squeezed the trigger of the water gun.

Jake also held her at gunpoint, but his eyes were alight with mischief. They both wore cowboy hats, bandanas tied around their necks, brown vests with a sheriff star pinned to the chest, plaid shirts, holsters belted around their middles, blue jeans and cowboy boots. They looked adorable in their outfits.

"If you'll come along peaceable, Ma'am," Tom continued, "we'd appreciate it. I'd hate to fill you full of lead."

Jane, with her hands raised above her head, looked past the two ominous figures on her doorstep and down the darkened driveway to where the minivan was parked and waiting under the streetlamp. Greg sat at the wheel with Caroline in the passenger seat. In the very back, a pouting Amy was clearly visible. Even though she had her head turned away from the scene at Jane's door, the slumped shoulders said Amy did not approve of this expedition. Jane turned her attention back to a friendly Boskell.

"I don't know what I did, Sheriff," complained Jane to the small officer of the law.

"Dad, I mean the judge, said you'd watered down the drinks at your saloon," answered Tom.

"And cheated at cards," added Jake with a gleeful grin and a vigorous nod. His hat slipped forward and, in true cowboy form, he used the point of his gun to push it back on his head.

Just what nonsense was Greg Boskell up to now? She looked again at the van. Greg and Caroline motioned her to hurry.

58

"May I get my purse and lock up?" she asked Tom.

The boys looked at each other in puzzlement. This must not have been part of the script they'd rehearsed.

Tom took the initiative. "Okay, Ma'am, but remember, we'll shoot if you try to escape."

"Yes, Sir," she answered, and quickly grabbed her purse, a jacket, and locked the door as she closed it.

They kept their pistols trained on her all the way down the driveway. Caroline hopped out of her seat and clambered over the console to sit in the back. Greg reached across to push open the front door.

"Good work, men," he said to his boys. "The West will soon be safe for honest citizens. Get in, Ma'am," he ordered Jane gruffly. "You're on your way to serve time behind bars."

The boys giggled and leapt into the backseat, sliding the door closed behind them.

"Buckle up," hollered the judge and pulled away from the curb.

"Do you like our costumes?" asked Jake. "They're for the party at church."

Jane turned slightly in her seat to peer back at her captors.

"For the Halloween thing?" she asked.

"Not Halloween," corrected Caroline. "It's something for us to do instead of trick-or-treating. It's safe."

"But it's still a lot of fun," assured Tom.

"Your costumes are great. Doesn't everybody have to go as cowboys?" She had read something about it in the bulletin.

"You can be an Indian, or a miner, or anything from the old West in the Denver area," said Caroline.

"I didn't think it was tonight," said Jane, a bit confused.

"No, it's next week. We're just going to the ice cream place."

"Are you guys crazy?" objected Jane. "It's thirty degrees out. We're going to have a big freeze tonight."

"Now who do you think is crazy, kids?" asked Greg. "The lady does not object to getting arrested by two fine lawmen but does object to ice cream."

"She's crazy," the boys echoed.

"Greg, I don't see this as ice cream weather," explained the prisoner.

Greg briefly looked over at her and grinned that crooked smile she found so hard to ignore.

"I have always felt compassion for the businessman who is at the whim of the thermometer," he explained. "Those poor people at the ice cream shop surely get lonely when the temperature drops. Haven't you seen the Maytag service man ad? Hasn't his plight of loneliness touched your heart? Can't you see that the same desolation must fall upon the isolated individuals whose lifelong work is to scoop ice cream? I can't buy washers very often, but I can do my bit to relieve the distress that is the lot of ice cream scoopers in our fair city." He ended his dramatic monologue and a cheer arose from the backseats.

Jane grinned in response.

"You needn't worry, Ma'am," he continued. "As the old saying goes, 'you can lead a horse to water, but you can't make him drink.' In this case, it would be that you can lead the prisoner to the ice cream, but you can't make her lick."

The giggles in the backseat showed the children appreciated their father's humor.

"Don't you worry," returned she who was accused of watering drinks and cheating at cards. "I can lick anything that's put before me." She turned a mockingly threatening eye upon the lawmen. "And given the chance, I'll lick two uppity sheriffs."

"I'm a marshal," claimed Jake.

"Then, I'll lick one uppity sheriff and one uppity marshal."

At the ice cream shop, they were the only customers and the boys told the girls behind the counter how they had arrested Miss Freedman.

"Then she should have an ice cream bar, actually two, so you can say she's been put behind bars," suggested the clerk.

Tom laughed and explained the pun to Jake.

"She can have anything she wants," Greg told the boys who were contemplating making their prisoner eat the bars.

Caroline joined in the fun, but Amy studiously looked through the glass at the big tubs of ice cream displayed as if choosing her flavor was utmost on her mind. After they ordered, the four children sat at one table on the spinning pink stools, and Greg and Jane sat at another.

"I assume, Judge," said Jane, "that this was done at your initiative."

"Yep," he admitted. "We were driving out of the subdivision, right by your house when the inspiration hit me. We circled the block as I rehearsed the boys in their parts. They're hams. I knew they'd get a kick out of it."

"I'll have you know they did an excellent job. I was shivering in my boots."

He grinned and looked over his shoulder at his happy crew. His eye caught Amy's sullen face, and he frowned.

Jane didn't want to get caught in a discussion of his eldest daughter so she asked, "Does the church do this Halloween thing every year?"

"Uh-huh," he answered rather vaguely. "The theme's always the Old West, and they've accumulated some great games. They even have a mock jail. You can pay the sheriffs to arrest anyone there, and then the prisoners plead from the jail to passersby to bail them out. The money goes to missions. Would you like to go with us this year?"

"No, thanks."

"I know, you have to stay home with the puppies," Greg supplied her excuse. "Why do you think we brought you at gunpoint tonight? You're not in the habit of saying yes."

"I did picnic in the park," reminded Jane.

"You were coerced," reminded Greg.

Jane shrugged and was saved from answering by the approach of Jake, who'd finished his cone and wore the evidence around his mouth. Jane grabbed him, both arms tightly around his waist.

"Now, I've got you, Sheriff," she exclaimed.

"I'm the marshal," giggled Jake.

"Marshal," said Jane, "I'm going to lick you. From the looks of you, I can get a full second helping off your cheeks." She stuck out her tongue and loomed toward his cheeks. He dissolved into a wiggling, laughing polecat.

Suddenly she released him, allowing him to sink to the floor. "On second thought," she explained, "I'm not that fond of the flavor you picked. I'll have to lick you another day."

Jake, still laughing, scrambled away on his knees and joined the other table. Jane looked up to see a smile on Amy's face, but as their eyes met, the smile faded and the girl deliberately turned away.

Greg laughed too. Jane quickly turned toward him hoping he hadn't noticed his daughter's action.

"So," he said, "you'll go with us to the roundup?"

"No," she said firmly but with a smile on her lips, "I will not."

"You're a stubborn woman, Miss Freedman."

"I'm a happy, contented, career woman, Mr. Boskell."

They returned her to the house, the judge proclaiming she was out on bail. Jane prettily thanked them for arresting her and taking her to jail. At their father's instruction, the boys escorted her to the door and waited until she had unlocked her door and stepped in. She waved to those in the van as she said good night to the boys. Greg lifted his hand in a farewell gesture, but he shook his head sadly over his inability to put Miss Jane Freedman at ease. Perhaps he should let some other Christian brother or sister step forward to fill the gap. Thing was, she was intriguing, and he hadn't found a woman intriguing in over four years.

ten

"Would you care to explain?" Greg looked down at Jane where she sat at a long table with several other women selling game tickets for the roundup. It was right inside the door of the activity center, and Greg handed over three dollars to purchase the tickets for his children. Amy was not with him.

"I said I wouldn't come with you," Jane answered the implied part of the question. "I didn't say I wouldn't be here."

The children reached across the table to get their hands stamped and ten tickets. They chattered away, happy to see their friend who had the puppies. They started to take off, and Greg stopped them for last-minute instructions. He ended with one last warning to stay out of trouble and a meeting place for lunch. They excitedly waved their hands and Jane turned to the next group. Three families later, she looked up to see Greg still stood there observing her.

"Greg, I hadn't intended to come, but someone called and asked if I'd man the front ticket table for two hours and so here I am." She turned away to speak to the next person entering. She was annoyed to find him still there after that person had gone through.

"Go away, Greg," she ordered softly, not wishing the ladies on either side of her to hear what she said.

"Will you have lunch with us?"

"No," she answered and deliberately turned to the next person.

He moved away and she sighed her relief.

Just after one o'clock, she stood up from her post and said good-bye to the two friendly ladies she'd worked beside. She wore the most Western thing she owned, a denim dress. Some of the outfits around her were really spectacular, and she decided to roam through the crowd to look at the people and the activities going on. She had only taken a few steps when one of the elders approached her.

"Good day to you, Miss Freedman." He doffed his Stetson.

"Hello, Mr. Wiley. I see you're one of the sheriffs."

"Yes, Ma'am," he answered with a twinkle in his eye, "and I have a warrant for your arrest."

By this time, Jane had witnessed several arrests. The jail was a crude structure made of two-by-fours painted black, and the occupants looked to be having a tremendous amount of fun. Anyone could buy a warrant naming any person present. The person was incarcerated in the mock jail. The prisoners begged their friends passing by to bail them out. It was against the rules to pay the bail out of your own money. All the money went to missionaries in Papua New Guinea.

"Who's having me arrested?" she asked, knowing what the answer would be.

"Greg Boskell," Sheriff Wiley responded.

"The charge?"

"Evading lunch," he grinned at her, took her by the elbow, and escorted her to the flimsy door that held the prisoners. The other prisoners greeted her enthusiastically. They asked her if she'd brought a file or smuggled a gun into the lockup. She responded as cheerfully as she could, but a part of her seethed in anger. Did this man not understand the word "no"?

Before long she saw his innocently smiling face outside the bars. She deliberately turned away and asked her Sunday school teacher as he passed by to help her with her bail. He joked with her as he handed her a dollar bill. Now she only needed four more. One of the ladies she'd just worked with passed and she gained another dollar toward her freedom. Several of her fellow prisoners raised their bail money and attained their release. More members of the congregation were pushed jokingly into the cell and began calling to the crowd to help them out.

Jane looked over her shoulder to where Greg leaned against

the wall. Her anger surged, but she made an effort to hide it. She turned a cold shoulder his direction and reached out to grab the arm of the next man who passed.

"Sir," she exclaimed in a heavy Southern accent. "I don't know you, Sir, but I ask you to kindly take pity on me. I have been falsely accused and placed in this wretched jail by a man who has only evil in his heart. Why, I believe that while I am incarcerated in this cell, he plans to steal the deed to the ranch left to me by my dearly departed father. The ranch is all that my widowed mother and my fifteen little brothers and sisters have. You look like such a fine upstanding citizen. Surely you can spare three dollars to bail out this innocent maid, so that I can rush back to the ranch and help fend off the villain who would steal my family's home."

The man chortled and pulled out his wallet. Jane soon had the money and she was free. She gave the bailiff another five dollars and bought a warrant for Greg Boskell.

"Charge?" asked the man playing court clerk.

"Scoundrel," said Jane, and scurried to the door, knowing she had to get out while the sheriff arrested her nemesis and before he could coerce bail from his friends.

☙

"I called to apologize," Greg's voice sounded tired. It was ten o'clock and the roundup had been in full swing since eleven that morning.

Jane wondered how long he had stayed there with his gang. She had glimpsed Amy helping at the cake walk. Had the teenager given him more trouble? It was none of her business, but she wasn't mad at him anymore. She'd cooled off shortly after she'd gotten home. During the afternoon, she'd fought the urge to go back to church to be a part of the fun. After all, Greg wasn't a lecher. He just wanted her to mix with people. She had to admit, she wasn't much of a mixer, and at times she would like to be more involved. That kind of thinking was dangerous, but during the early hours of the evening, she decided to be firm with Greg, but not antagonistic.

"I could see you were mad," he went on. "I meant it as a joke, and I guess I didn't consider your feelings."

"I got over it," explained Jane, "but thanks for the apology. Did your kids enjoy the day?"

"Yes," he answered, obviously glad to have that hurdle over.

Jane snuggled down under her bed covers and put her head down on the pillow. She had just about finished her book but, at the moment, was more interested in what the children had done at the church.

"Caroline met up with some of her friends, and I hardly saw her except when she needed another dollar for tickets. The boys I keep closer tabs on since they seem more adept at finding trouble. Did you see the pony rides out back? That was new this year and they each tried it, but I take them horseback riding on what they term 'real horses,' so they declared the ponies were for little kids.

"Amy was in her element. I think she'd signed up to work half a dozen booths. She seemed to have more fun than I've seen her have for a long time. We didn't leave until eight, but I didn't have a lick of trouble getting them in bed."

"I'm glad it was successful."

"They look forward to it every year. The next big to-do is the Thanksgiving Pie Party. The men try to outdo each other in wearing outrageous ties. They have a lie contest, where some of the church's best storytellers tell tall tales. The children enjoy that, and so do I. The ladies have a "buy" corner where they sell Christmas bazaar type items. Kathy always had a lot of contributions to that."

"Will you tell me a little bit about Kathy?" asked Jane.

"Sure." He paused to decide where to begin. "You know she was a twin. They were Kathleen and Katherine. My Kathy was Kathleen and Kate is Katherine. They were identical. Originally, I went out with Kate who wasn't impressed with our first date. So, the next time I picked her up, it was Kathy standing in for her. I knew within two minutes that the other twin was my date. That always amazed them that I never could be fooled as to which one was which."

He paused but instead of jumping in with a conversation filler, Jane waited. Greg continued.

"They were both artists. Kate is more of a salesperson, so she handled that end of the business. Their studio is the whole third floor of this house."

"What kind of art did they do?" asked Jane.

"Everything. They painted pictures on canvas, saw blades, rocks, bottles, anything. They sculpted with clay. They designed and made jewelry. Kathy designed clothes for awhile but she lost interest in that."

"Sounds pretty interesting. They're extremely talented."

"It's hard to keep the tenses straight, isn't it?" asked Greg with a chuckle in his voice. "Kathy was talented. Kate is talented."

"It must be odd to have the identical twin of your wife popping in and out," said Jane wondering aloud.

"I ceased to see them as identical," explained Greg. "They moved differently, talked differently, even had a different expression when they concentrated. Their eyes were worlds apart in many ways, yet I seemed to be the only one who saw it.

"It's funny. The mannerisms that they shared are the ones that Kathy used to drive me crazy with. The little things she did that I overlooked because I loved her, Kate does and I want to strangle her for them."

"Like what?"

"Whistling through her teeth. Leaving the tea bag on the counter. Cleaning a paint brush on her shirtsleeve. Twirling her hair around a finger when she's about to tell me something I'm not going to like."

"All very heinous crimes," commented Jane. "Is Kate good with the kids?"

"In about the same way Kathy was," answered Greg. "She loved the kids, but her art really came first, and if she was involved in a project she pretty much ignored them. We had a housekeeper and a nanny back then. It caused some friction between us, but when she did focus on the children she was marvelous. She made up for days of neglect. I kept saying they needed a quantity of quality time, and she'd just laugh. The house ran smoothly. The children were happy. I was making 'much ado about nothing.' "

"Where were the housekeeper and the nanny on the day Kathy died?"

"They were together in Topeka, Kansas. They were second cousins attending the same family reunion. That was one of the reasons nobody panicked about the children. We were all so used to Mrs. White and Miss Burney being with the children. In the shock of what was happening, the details of who was with the children just got lost."

"When did they leave your employ?" asked Jane.

"Believe it or not, they both got married. First the nanny, Miss Burney, and then Mrs. White, who was sixty if she was a day."

"And you never replaced them?"

"Well, we tried, but no one worked out, and it was an expense I couldn't afford without Kathy's income, plus my own business didn't do so well for awhile after Kathy died. I couldn't keep my mind on it."

They talked for awhile longer about his business, her business with Mark Banner's Designs in Antiquity, living in Denver, and her life in Maryland. They talked about how she'd received her training and his one-time ambition to be an architect, which had been put aside when opportunities to be the builder instead of the designer kept him on the path he'd taken.

"Do you regret not following a different path?" she asked.

"No, but I regret talking your ear off. Do you realize it is after one in the morning?"

Jane glanced over at the clock "Well, I guess I won't be at the early service tomorrow. Good night, Greg. I'm glad you called."

"So am I. I haven't talked like this in ages. It was relaxing. Good night."

eleven

Whatever service Greg went to the next day it was not the same one as Jane. She had looked for him, then chastised herself for wanting to catch even a glimpse of his smiling face. She knew from the bulletin and announcements that many church people would be on the premises finishing the cleanup after the previous day's activities. She toyed with the idea of hanging around supposedly to help but in reality hoping that Greg and his family would show up.

She'd put the scheme aside. She had a pile of work to finish writing up on the newest proposal. The problem with working at home was that she was less rigid about working "office" hours and tended to fit her projects in around playing with the puppies and Caroline's afternoon visits. Jane sighed and sat at her desk rummaging through the sketches and written plans. Interaction with the Boskells had spoiled her. What was wrong with spending a beautiful Sunday afternoon at her designs? Nothing! With intensity of purpose, Jane tackled her assignment and banished any thoughts of the Boskells. At least she tried.

She didn't find out until the next day that the family had spent Sunday with their Grandma Standish. Her assistant with the puppies showed up promptly after school let out and was full of news.

"Where are the boys?" Jane asked, surprising herself that she was sorry they hadn't appeared.

"They went to Billy Newcomb's birthday party." Caroline screwed up her face in an expressive disdain of boys.

"Amy's grounded," continued her town crier. "It's the first time ever."

Jane couldn't think what to say. Reminding herself that it

was *not* her business, she refrained from asking why. She needn't have bothered. Caroline more than willingly filled her in on the details without being prompted by questions.

"She wanted to wear a dress to school that Dad says is too. . . I can't remember the word. But Dad said no and Amy said he was all mixed up in his head because he'd been without sex for four years, and he got real quiet and then sent her to her room. He went up to talk to her later, and all you have to do with Dad is admit you're wrong and say you're sorry and things like that.

"Amy must have been mule-headed 'cause Dad said. . . well, Dad said she was mule-headed, and so she can't go anywhere for a week or until she comes to her senses and he may have her barricaded in her room until she's twenty-one!"

"I'm sure your dad and Amy will work it out," assured Jane.

"Miss Freedman, Amy *never* gets in trouble. Never!" Caroline looked concerned and Jane went to put an arm around her, sitting beside her on the bed where Caroline had been keeping her eyes on the puppies as she talked.

"Sometimes it's really good to get in trouble, Caroline," said Jane. "Amy has a problem that she's keeping hidden, probably something about growing up and not having your mom there to help. If she didn't get into trouble, your dad would never know the problem is there, and he couldn't help. Now he has a chance to figure it out, and what we should do is pray for God to help him."

"Wouldn't God help him anyway?" Caroline asked.

Jane nodded, thinking over what was the right thing to say about prayer. "Of course, He's always willing to help His children, but He likes prayer. He likes us to be concerned for one another, and He likes us to turn to Him.

"It really is all for our own benefit. Each time we pray we connect to the Creator of the universe. We get stronger because we care and because we're trusting Him."

Jane remembered something Mrs. Grehurst had said in the Bible club she'd gone to more than a dozen years before.

"How do you spell 'pray,' Caroline?"

"That's easy," she replied. "P-R-A-Y."

"Right," said Jane. "A teacher once told me to remember this: P stands for *please,* because God likes us to say 'please' and 'thank you' just like our parents do. It is nicer than whining or demanding. It's also because God is pleased when we do the right thing, and because like a gentleman, God never forces people to do what they should. It's almost like He says, 'Please do what's right because I don't want you to come to harm.' "

"Cool," observed Caroline.

"The R is for *remembering,* because all the good things you know about God and all the things you've learned about right and wrong don't do you a bit of good if you don't remember them. Sometimes people act hastily, before they think things out, before they remember. Talking to God in prayer is an excellent way to think things through. He's our counselor and guides our thoughts, if we remember."

"A's next," said Caroline helpfully.

"A is for *always.* Can you guess why always is important?"

"Because acting like a Christian *sometimes* is not as good as *always?*"

"That's the general idea," agreed Jane. "Always turn to God. Always remember how great He is. Always remember He loves you. Always do what He says. There are a lot of 'always,' but you really summed it up. Always act like a Christian."

"The Y," Caroline said eagerly.

"Y is for *yield,*" said Jane. "That one is a little tougher."

"We talked about yielding in Sunday school. It means doing what God wants instead of what you want. You give up what you want if it's wrong and do what God wants instead."

"A perfect answer, Caroline." Jane hugged the girl. "You're very wise for your age." Caroline grinned under her praise.

"Please remember always yield." Jane put it together.

"That's good advice, huh?" asked Caroline.

"Very good advice, and just think, I learned that about fifteen years ago and I still remember it."

"Are you going to the Thanksgiving Pie Party?" asked Caroline abruptly.

Jane considered trying to avoid it and figured it would cause a strain between her and Caroline's father, so she smiled and gave in immediately instead of trying to fight the inevitable.

"Yes," she answered. "And soon after that, the puppies will begin to go to their new homes."

Caroline beamed and picked up Princess for a special cuddle.

"Tell me," said Jane. "When you wished upon that puppy was the wish that she would be yours?"

Caroline grinned mischievously. "No," she admitted. "That was maybe a side wish, and I'm glad it came true, but the big wish is still coming. I promise I'll tell you when it comes true."

Jane learned from Caroline that her father was finishing up a project and therefore would not be around the house much for a couple of weeks.

"It has to do with inspections and things. Dad gets what he calls real prideful about passing the inspections. He's in a real bad mood if the building doesn't make it."

Jane was not surprised that she didn't see much of Greg for the two weeks before the Pie Party, but he kept reminding Jane through Caroline that he and the boys would pick her up and take her to the shindig.

❧

"Just look at it, Caroline." Jane held out the pie for the girl's inspection. She'd followed the directions and put foil covers on the exposed pie crust rim; therefore, that part didn't look too bad. But a skin of black pumpkin crowned the custard filling.

Caroline shrugged. "It doesn't look so bad. Just peel off that burnt stuff and cover it with whipped cream. Aunt Kate does that all the time. She knows just what to do when things don't go right in the kitchen. If it's a dessert, she says you can fix it with either whipped cream or chocolate. If it's a vegetable, you disguise it with cheese, and if it's tough or salty meat, you chop it up and make it a sandwich filling."

"She sounds like my kind of cook," said Jane with a sigh. Her failed culinary effort still sat ugly upon the counter.

"Daddy's a better cook. He'll show you how if you want him to." Caroline studied Jane's face. She reached out and gently touched her arm. "Don't worry. Just put lots of whipped cream on it and Jake and Tom will love it."

She scooted off her stool and made for the patio to play with the boys and the puppies. Jane went to the refrigerator and pulled out a can of pressurized whip cream. Carefully, with a sharp knife and fork, she peeled off the offending burnt layer. Underneath, the pumpkin looked almost okay. She wasn't quite sure it was firm enough, but hoped the whipped cream would cover that deficiency as well. At least at the church pie party, there ought to be plenty of pies so that hers wouldn't stand out. It could be lost in the crowd. And for added measure, she'd be sure to put it on the back edge of the dessert table.

She pressed her finger against the nozzle and began covering the disgraceful pie, going around and around from the outside to the center. That looked fairly good so she added another smaller layer and then a third so it mounted to a peak at the center.

She stood back to admire the effect.

"Very nice," said Greg behind her.

She jumped and her finger tightened against the nozzle sending a spurt of white foam into the air. It hit a cabinet door, stuck for a moment, and then began to slide down.

She grabbed a paper towel and leaped to catch it before it fell on the counter below. Greg laughed.

"You scared me," she scolded.

"You need a little excitement in your life."

"Oh, I do?"

"Yes," Greg said emphatically. "A little chaos, a little disorder, a little spontaneity. Is the pie burnt?"

"Yes," she answered sharply.

He laughed again. "We have a lot of whipped cream at our

house. Kate is artistic on canvas, but she does not excel in the kitchen."

"Why do you think a person needs a little disorder?" Jane asked to change the subject.

"I didn't say a person, I said you."

"Okay. Why do I need a little disorder?" She turned her back to him and picked up the washrag that hung over the divider in the double sink. She ran warm water through it, squeezed, and began wiping down the cabinet surface for any stray cream. Then she continued on to the spotless countertops.

"Your house is perfect, Jane. It reflects your taste and style but it doesn't reflect your person. There are no tissues indicating you have a cold."

"I don't have a cold."

"That's just an example. If you did have a cold, would you leave the tissues lying about?"

"No."

"Your coat is in the closet instead of draped over a chair. Everything is in its place. There's no room for the little variances that make life interesting. You need to relax and let go. Be a little outrageous."

Jane carefully rinsed out the washrag and hung it neatly back in its place as he spoke. Her childhood had been full of variances, outrageous surprises, and spontaneous disasters. She hadn't found them worthy of praise.

"Jane, we really enjoy your company, but sometimes I feel like you're just watching, not really entering into the activity, whatever it is."

Jane moved back to look at her disfigured pie carefully camouflaged to be acceptable. Her life was like that. She smiled at her whimsical analogy. Her life was a soupy pumpkin chiffon pie with the burnt layer discarded and cosmetically covered with socially acceptable whipped cream. She picked the pie up and balanced it in the palm of her hand. She should get out the pie carrier and seal it up to put in the fridge. She didn't want it to get too warm before they left for the church. The filling was already in trouble. If it got warm, it would give up any attempt to be set up and run all over the counter.

"You are a wonderful person," Greg continued. "I'd just like to see you do something out of the ordinary, something impulsive."

She whirled around and, with remarkably good aim, smashed the pie directly into Greg's face. She pulled back her hand, and the tin pie plate stuck for a moment before sliding off and hitting the floor with a muffled clatter.

Greg blinked and his eyes appeared in the middle of the mess.

"I didn't mean to do that," Jane gasped. "I don't know. . . I just. . . You said. . ."

Greg licked his lips.

"That's a start. That was certainly unexpected." He licked his lips again, and she could see the grin.

"I'm so sorry," she said, grabbing the towel hanging from the ring beside the sink. He caught her hand before she could wipe off the evidence of her spontaneity.

"Oh no you don't," he exclaimed. "Now you must receive retribution." His voice alerted her to some plan that she would most likely find disagreeable.

"What are you thinking?" she asked.

"Revenge." He took hold of her other wrist and backed her against the counter.

"What are you going to do?"

"Share." He looked her in the eyes, and she saw pure mischief gleaming in those blue, whipped cream surrounded orbs. He began by rubbing his cheeks against hers, one side and then the other, while she protested with screeches and giggles. His forehead smeared across hers, leaving a mass of filling and cream. Then, he hit her chin with his. Not satisfied, he nuzzled into her neck and up against her ear. She laughed uncontrollably by the time he got to her mouth and then she stopped.

She hadn't expected him to kiss her. His hands let go of her, and his arms went around her waist pulling her closer.

She did nothing to resist. It was the most heavenly kiss she'd ever experienced. It was the giggling that interrupted them. Not theirs, but the giggles of Caroline, Jake, and Tom.

Jake and Tom had the audacity to fall on the floor and roll. Caroline just held her sides. Suggums and the puppies stormed into the kitchen and started licking up all the pie debris from the floor.

"Oh no!" cried Jane. "Pick up the puppies! They'll be sick." With her face still covered with pie, she scooped up two puppies. She had to hold them away from her face as she rushed to put them back in the pen. They turned their faces to her and desperately strained little pink tongues to taste the forbidden yummy. Their lightning-fast tongues darted in and out, making an all-out effort to reach just one inch farther to where the cream clung to her cheeks. Greg picked up two more and transferred them with similar trouble. Caroline snatched the last.

"Quick, get Suggums outside!" Jane called, returning from the other room. Jake picked up the dog, slipped on the slick floor and fell. There he laughed again so hard that he couldn't stand. He held a squirming Suggums in the air until Tom had the presence of mind to grab her and haul her to the patio door. The feast available inside was too compelling though, and Suggums slipped between his feet before he could drag the door closed. Caroline and Greg came back to help, and they managed to banish the gluttonous dog while Jane went after towels.

Jane reappeared from the bathroom and handed towels around to initiate the cleanup. She and Greg both stooped down mopping the floor. He leaned over and whispered in her ear, "That's the sweetest kiss I've ever had."

She tried to glare at him, but it dissolved into a grin. It was certainly the sweetest in her book as well.

twelve

"I came to report on the puppy's adjustment to her new home," Greg said as he stood on her front step.

Jane shook her head. "No need. Caroline popped in after school for half-a-sec to tell me all's well. She couldn't stay longer because she had to rush home."

"Well," said Greg, "I had kind of hoped to stay for more than half-a-sec."

She allowed him to pass.

He handed over his hat and heavy jacket, which she placed on the bench. She stood in the hall with her arms crossed over her middle and a dubious look on her face.

"Were you going to offer me coffee or anything?" Greg asked, a smile lurking in his eyes.

"I'm not about to offer you anything at all, Mr. Boskell," she answered in a friendly tone, but definitely without enthusiasm for his visit.

He nodded. "I didn't really come to tell you about Princess."

"I figured."

"I came to kiss you," he admitted. "Without the pumpkin pie and the audience."

"That would not be a good idea," said Jane, visibly tightening her arms in a protective gesture.

"Could we have a cup of coffee and discuss it?" Greg sounded hopeful.

"No," was the answer.

He looked at her. She was gorgeous. At times she looked too much like a model for his taste, but that was just a facade. The tailored clothes, the precise makeup were part of her job. He'd seen her in more relaxed atmospheres and she was beautiful in a very clean and comfortable way. She had a lovely smile. Her laugh was charming. She was even good to his kids, while she kept claiming she had no interest in the next generation beyond the nodding acquaintance she could not avoid. But, best of all, she made him feel alive. He wanted to protect her and cherish her. And she wanted him out the front door as quickly as possible.

"Look, Greg," she began, "I've made no secret of the fact that I do not want to be anything but a friend to you. I am not even remotely a candidate for the next mother of the Boskell clan. And I don't believe in casual physical relationships. So your coming here to kiss me is rather pointless."

She let go of her arms, ceasing to hug herself in that extremely defensive posture and for a moment, Greg was hopeful. However, she clenched her hands together and held them in front of her at waist height. Not a more promising body language.

He smiled warmly and spoke softly, trying to disarm her.

"I enjoyed our last kiss and I thought you did, too."

"Yes, I did," she proclaimed. "In the same way I enjoy the antics of the Three Stooges."

"I detected something more than slapstick comedy," insisted Greg.

"It was the whipped cream, Greg," Jane was equally insistent. "Or the pumpkin custard. Yes, I'm sure the pumpkin flavor added that certain exotic quality that anyone might mistake for. . ."

She hesitated and looked down at the floor. He took a step closer and put a finger under her chin to raise her face. Their eyes met.

"For," Greg finished her sentence, "passion."

Jane's lips pressed together and she darted to the side, hurrying down the hall and away from her tormentor.

The tormentor followed and was greeted with enthusiasm by Suggums, the traitor.

When the royal exchange of pleasantries was finished, Jane spoke up, defensive, as usual.

"Greg," she spoke sharply, "you're only the third man who has ever kissed me. That obviously means that I'm not really a good judge of such things. However, I have taken care of my life for a long time, and I am able to judge what will benefit me, and what constitutes a threat to my very peace of mind."

"Only two before me?" Greg smiled and closed the distance between them again. "Tell me about your first kiss."

"My first kiss?" Jane asked nervously.

"Uh-huh." Greg nodded and stopped moving, pushing his hands into his jeans pockets.

Jane watched him warily. At least he wasn't coming any closer. If it would keep him at a distance, she would talk.

"It was in high school. My first date. Denny Salchenbacher took me to a movie. I sat two tables over from Denny Salchenbacher for six months in the school cafeteria. I'd watched him eat for six months. Not that I really wanted to watch. I actually tried not to, but it was fascinating in a grotesque way. He shoveled his food. Almost like automation. He scooped with one hand, brought it up to his mouth, pressed it in, and swallowed while the other hand brought up the next load. He devoured everything from donuts to pizza in the same manner. There was the bizarre fascination in that any minute he might choke. He never did.

"Anyway, after we went to see a movie, we went to a hamburger joint where I got to observe the eating procedure up close. I decided his mother had never told him to chew with his mouth closed. She'd never had a chance. He never chewed. He skipped that part and went straight to the swallow. His Adam's apple was way over-developed in his ostrich-scrawny neck. Probably from the exercise of swallowing masses of never-been-chewed food.

"We didn't talk much over the hamburgers, and then, he took me home. On the doorstep he grabbed my head, just like he'd grabbed a double cheeseburger with bacon about thirty-five minutes before. He pulled me toward his mouth, and my life passed before my eyes just like they say it does for a person who's drowning.

"I knew in about three seconds I was going to be swallowed. His face hit mine at full force, and by some miracle, my life was spared with only minor injuries."

During her talk, Greg sank onto the couch and began laughing. Jane relaxed and sat down on the same couch but at the other end. Suggums jumped into her lap, and Jane petted the silky fur, smiling to herself over the fiasco of her first kiss.

When Greg could speak again, he asked about the second kiss.

"That was in college. I worked in a department store selling shoes. In the back, rows and rows of narrow shelves stored all the different sized shoes matching the floor models. One day I was back there during a lightning storm and the lights went out."

Jane paused. "I guess I should tell you about my coworker, Andrew Whittiker, before we continue. Andy was greasy—not dirty greasy, but greasy by design. He used some sort of hair gel that slicked back his black hair. Then he wore one of those really thin mustaches that just made a hairy line across his upper lip. It looked like someone had taken a permanent marker and underlined his nose. As a matter of fact, it was a remarkable nose, one worthy of being distinguished by an underline. Aquiline is the polite term for a beak with a hump.

"Andy was kind of a nice kid, but a little short on social skills. Once he got over creating his image and just became Andy the regular guy, he was going to be okay. So, I was friendly with him. That's a mistake. Never get too friendly with a guy who is defining his image." Jane sighed over the memory.

"Back to the storage room and the lights out. I heard a noise, and Andy spoke up saying not to worry, it was just him. So, I wasn't worried until I discovered that in the dark, he had grown six more arms to make him Octopus Man. Kind of like a werewolf phenomenon, only it was the dark and the smell of shoe leather rather than the full moon that must have set him off. He grabbed me and proceeded to rain kisses upon my face. Actually, he only hit my lips once or twice and his hands were more of a concern to me at the time. I hardly noticed what his lips were doing until he licked my cheek. That's when I recalled a maneuver explained to me by my worldly-wise aunt Nelda.

"It worked, and I clung to the shelves knocking shoes and shoe boxes down on him as I stepped over his body and made my way out to the floor where I had enough time to regain my composure before the lights came back on."

"You're making it up," gasped Greg, holding his side and leaning forward as tears rolled down his cheeks.

"I am not," asserted Jane. "My last kiss was lubricated with pumpkin pie. How can you doubt that my previous experiences were any more conventional?"

"So what you have yet to experience is a normal kiss," said Greg, suddenly controlling his laughter and giving her a speculative look, "devoid of any threat to your life, not accompanied by superfluous hand action, and no added flavorings? In other words, a normal kiss."

Jane became wary and rose from the couch. "I'll fix you that cup of coffee." Maybe with a mug of hot coffee in his hands he might be less dangerous.

He followed her into the kitchen and stood resting against the doorjamb.

She measured out the coffee into the filter and filled the water tank. When she had turned on the brewer, she busied herself putting back the can of coffee grounds and getting out the mugs and various other things that might be needed when serving a cup of coffee. Unfortunately, she finished before the coffee did. She stood facing the counter watching it drip.

"Jane," Greg spoke softly behind her. She whirled around and was relieved to see that he was still in the same position against the door. The look in his eye, however, was not comforting. He straightened up and deliberately put both hands behind his back before stepping forward.

"Nice, slow, and gentle," he said as he progressed.

"Greg," she protested.

"No octopus hands," he reassured her. He stood inches away and leaned slowly, bringing his head down with the obvious intent of capturing the kiss he'd come for.

"No additives, artificial or otherwise," he whispered. His lips touched hers in a feathery light embrace. He backed off a bit and looked into her eyes before he again closed the space between them. This time, his lips lingered and moved gently against hers, tenderly caressing without any urgent demands. Again he backed off to look down into her upturned face. He waited until she opened her eyes to look at him, confusion apparent by the slight frown lines across her brow.

"Oh, Jane," he whispered, and still with his hands behind his back, he leaned forward, kissed her forehead, and then her temple, and trailed a line of soft kisses across her cheek back to her mouth. She responded, and his arms came out from behind his back. His hands went up to touch her shoulders but stopped and hovered next to her without touching. Just as he was about to encircle her with those eager arms, he kept his promise and tucked them back behind him.

But Jane had not made the promise, and Jane had never been kissed with such devotion. She leaned closer until she was pressed against him and her arms went around his waist. This time when he pulled back, she felt deserted. She did not want him to back away. She lowered her head and rested it against his chest. Slowly, she released her hold on him and leaned away.

"Go away, Greg," she pleaded in a whisper.

He kissed her once more, briefly, just touching his lips to the top of her head, and then turned away. She stood frozen as she listened to him go down the hall, pause to put on his coat, and open the door. When the door closed behind him, she let out a great sigh.

Well, Lord. That's gone and broken the dam. I hope You're going with me on this because I'm scared to death.

ॐ

When she stepped out of the shower, the phone was ringing,

and she rushed to the bed still dripping in a hastily donned robe and a towel swathed around her wet hair.

"Hello."

"I was afraid you wouldn't answer," Greg said.

"I was in the shower," she explained.

"Are you okay, Jane?" he asked.

"Yes, no, yes," she stuttered.

"Me, too." He chuckled. He took a deep breath and let it out slowly. "Jane. . ."

"Yes?"

"I'm going to tell you something, and I want you to hear me out."

"Okay."

"I want you to know at this very moment I love you. I've felt it growing for weeks. Right now I want to throw you over my shoulder and run to the preacher. But," he paused and searched for words. "But, that's how it was with Kathy, and it wasn't really right. We got along tolerably and there was a lot of affection, but God wasn't the center of our marriage. It wasn't a partnership before God. I grew spiritually and Kathy wasn't interested. Have you ever tried to drag someone else along your spiritual path? It doesn't work."

He paused again and Jane felt confident he didn't expect any words of wisdom from her. He was thinking through what he wanted to say. She sat patiently waiting on the edge of her bed, her robe wrapped around her like a cocoon. The towel hastily arranged about her wet head began to droop. She didn't mind. Her full attention focused on this man who an hour ago had awoken a part of her that had never seen the light of day, or a moonlit night, or stars reflected off a shimmering lake.

"I want to develop what we have together into more than a marriage between two people," he finally said. "I want it to be a heavenly relationship. God and two people."

Jane still didn't respond.

"I guess that sounds kind of idealistic, doesn't it?"

Jane nodded and then realized he couldn't see.

"I'm scared, Greg," she whispered.

"So am I, Honey," admitted Greg. "I don't want to be a shallow husband to you. You make me feel like I want to give it all. My optimistic side says finally God has brought me the woman of my dreams. The pessimistic side says, 'But you, Greg Boskell, are so one hundred percent human that you haven't got a prayer of getting this thing right even with a second chance and someone as wonderful as Jane.' I'm afraid this will all dwindle into a passable marriage when I have such great hopes for the sublime marriage."

"Let's just go slow, Greg," begged Jane. "I've never even met a man who tempted me to make that commitment. You knock me over every time you smile at me. I'm very insecure in my expectations of how I'll do with a family. Remember, I've zilch experience along those lines. If this is right, God will guide us, won't He?"

"Yes, He will." Greg was silent as if contemplating the next move. Suddenly his tone of voice shifted. "Okay. We go on as before but taking care to nourish the relationship. I want this to work, do you?"

Jane grinned. Now Greg sounded like he did when he conducted a business meeting.

"Yes," she said.

"Here's the game plan. We spend time together. We isolate problem areas. We discuss them. We pray. We give our love time to grow stronger."

"Agreed."

"You haven't said it."

She knew what he referred to.

"I love you, Greg. I've loved you since the night you sent your two lawmen after me and had me arrested on trumped-up charges."

thirteen

"May I bring Princess over to visit?" asked Caroline. Jane cradled the telephone against her ear and smiled. She'd missed the little girl's daily visits now that the puppy had gone home to her new owner. But things were going to be hectic today.

"I'd love that, Caroline, but I have to work today."

"It's Saturday, and you've gone to your office every day." Jane could hear the disappointment in her little friend's voice and could picture her lower lip beginning to push out in an adorable pout.

"I know, but we're opening a gallery in the mall, and I have to meet with some construction men this morning."

"Why can't you work at home like you used to?"

"That was just until the puppies were big enough to go to homes. I have just a short amount of time before the gallery opens. You wouldn't believe the oodles of things I have to attend to. I have to *be* there to work on most of them."

Jane could hear Caroline breathing into the phone. She knew the little girl had been to her house several times during the past week. She'd found notes on the front door and messages on her answering machine.

A heavy sigh came across the line. "Will you be working *all* day?"

"Yes, Caroline," she answered.

"Princess misses her mommy," Caroline explained. "She cries at night even when I hold her."

Mentally, Jane went over her to-do list for the day, hunting for something to move. Each item was important, unbudgeable.

"I'll see you tomorrow at church, Caroline." Jane pushed her hair back behind her ears. One of the things on the list was a haircut.

"Princess is lonely *today* and has been for a *week*." Caroline stressed the important words. Jane didn't need a degree in child psychology to figure it out. Time was what the little girl wanted. In this case, time together equaled attention.

If Caroline's voice had been a little more demanding, Jane probably would've been annoyed and therefore stood firm. Her little friend sounded lonely, not spoiled.

"I'll call you as soon as I get home," she promised, "and I'll try to hurry some things along."

"Hurray! Thank you, Miss Freedman."

"Right," Jane answered, trying to keep her tone cheerful while her thoughts battled over her constant dilemma. "I'll see you both later."

Why do I do that? Sure, it would be nice to spend more time with the Boskells. But I'm busy! I do enjoy the kids. Well, except Amy. I never thought little kids could be so entertaining. And Greg. Greg is improving. I'm getting to be more comfortable around him. Comfortable? I don't know if those zingy feelings I get when he smiles at me are all that comfortable. My tranquil lifestyle is shattered, she complained to herself as she headed down the hall to the bathroom. *My steady, even existence has been dumped in a tornado.*

She picked up her brush and grinned at her reflection in the mirror.

Maybe I can get my hair appointment changed to Monday.

❧

Later that afternoon, Jane draped her dry cleaning across the back of the living room sofa and kicked her shoes off.

"Hello, Suggums," she said in response to the dog's excited greeting. The clock on the mantel said 3:40. She plopped onto the couch, and Suggums launched herself into her lap to make sure Jane knew she was thoroughly welcome. "Missed me, huh?" Jane laughed as she rubbed the little dog vigorously. "Well, let me call Caroline, and you can have some more company."

By the time Caroline bounced through the door with

Princess on her leash, Jane had changed into designer jeans and a silk shirt.

"Daddy's cleaning up the house and throwing away a lot of junk," Caroline announced. She dropped down on her knees and scooped up Suggums to give her a big hug.

"Look what I bought today for Princess." Jane pulled a soft brush out of a plastic bag.

"Thanks," said Caroline, giving it a cursory glance, "but Daddy got me one already."

"Oh, this one is for here." Jane sat on the sofa and patted the place next to her inviting Caroline to join her. As soon as the dogs had calmed down from greeting each other, they jumped up on the laps provided. Caroline and Jane sat companionably brushing their pampered pets.

"Um," said Jane, "so, your dad is cleaning up. I seem to remember him saying something about the living room being a junk heap." She smiled at Caroline.

"A lot of it is Mom's art stuff. Daddy nags Aunt Kate to look through the stuff and haul it away before he throws it out."

"He wouldn't throw out her pictures!" Jane's face twisted in dismay. Her own sketches of designs were precious to her. She couldn't imagine some male deciding they were worthless and tossing them.

"No, it's not pictures," explained Caroline. Her answer caused Jane considerable relief, but Caroline was oblivious to her friend's emotions. "There're books and magazines and empty canvases and sketchbooks and boxes of letters. There's just a lot of junk."

"Can't you just move it up to the studio?" Without interrupting their conversation, Jane took the brush from Caroline's hand. She demonstrated for Caroline a better way to brush her puppy's tender ear and then handed the brush back.

"Daddy says no, there isn't room up there and most of it isn't valuable to anyone but Aunt Kate."

Princess bit the brush and Caroline laughed at her.

"Bad doggy," Jane said with calm firmness and pulled the

brush out of her reach. "No bites!" She winked at Caroline. "Don't let her get into bad habits."

"Okay," Caroline readily agreed. "Daddy says you're going to come to Grandma's for Thanksgiving."

Jane suppressed the shudder that came to her at the thought. It had taken some of Greg's best persuasive techniques to get her to agree to this plan.

"I'll be there in the evening. I had already planned to have lunch with Mr. and Mrs. Cooper before your dad invited me."

"I don't know who Mr. and Mrs. Cooper are," said Caroline.

"You'd recognize them if you saw them," assured Jane. "They're the old couple that sits right in the front row on the organ side of the church. She always wears a hat and he has a cane with a duck's head on the top."

"Them!" Caroline exclaimed with her eyes popping out of her head. "They're *old!*"

Jane nodded, grinning. Indeed, the Coopers were very old.

"I've done this for years, Caroline. I've never had anyone to celebrate Thanksgiving, Christmas, New Year's, Easter, any of the holidays with. So, I pick an old couple in the church and take them out to dinner."

"You're going to have Thanksgiving dinner in a restaurant!" Her eyes grew bigger at this revelation. "Miss Freedman, you can come to our house. *Nobody* has Thanksgiving in a restaurant."

"Actually, quite a few people do, Caroline, or the restaurants wouldn't be open. Anyway, this year I've already made plans, and I'll come to your grandma's after I drop the Coopers at their home."

"When will that be?" Caroline accepted Jane's plans begrudgingly.

"Around four o'clock."

"Grandma makes wonderful stuffing," said Caroline in a last attempt to bribe her friend into changing her mind.

"Maybe next year I can eat with your family."

Caroline brightened at this. "Yes, next year and the year

after and the year after."

Jane looked carefully at the little girl's beaming face.

"Suppose we just take one year at a time," suggested Jane.

"Okay," Caroline agreed without further argument, but that look of bliss did not diminish one iota.

The doorbell rang.

"I'll get it." Caroline jumped from the sofa and ran down the hall with two furry beasts yapping and circling her legs.

"It's the boys," she yelled back, her voice clearly indicating that the visitors were unimportant and unwelcome.

"Hey!" said Thomas. "I brought you something from Mike's party."

Jane had joined them in the hall. She stood watching the three children, amazed at how quickly she'd come to enjoy their company. She watched to see what a little brother would think to bring his sister from a party.

"What?" asked Caroline, her hands on her hips and a doubting look in her eyes.

"This!" squealed Tom and he thrust a wiggling rubber snake in her face. Caroline shrieked, the dogs barked, and Jacob howled with laughter. Thomas continued to dangle the offensive toy in his sister's face, and Jane suddenly thought, *Turnabout is fair play.*

Dramatically, she collapsed against the wall and slid down as if in a dead faint. The children immediately quieted, but the dogs continued to yap. When Suggums noticed Jane slumped against the door frame, she barreled across the floor and pounced on her. Jane didn't move.

"What happened?" asked a small voice.

"You scared her," asserted Caroline.

"She fainted?" asked the same quivering voice.

Swift footsteps approached, and Jane felt someone lean over her, someone who smelled vaguely of little boy sweat and old sneakers. She tensed and sprang, grabbing Thomas at the same time she yelled, "Gotcha!" Thomas fell against her and she rolled him to the floor beside her. Her fingers found tender ticklish spots beneath his arms. He squealed, the dogs barked, and Jacob and Caroline howled with laughter. Jane pulled Thomas into a firm hug and whispered in his ear.

"Look at them laughing at us."

Thomas gulped back his giggles and grinned at his siblings standing over them, holding their sides and laughing.

"Let's get 'em," Jane said. Tom nodded and the two became a team, launching an attack on the unsuspecting Jacob and Caroline. Tom tackled his sister, but Jake eluded Jane, and she had to scramble to her feet to chase him down. She caught him in the living room and threw him on the sofa. She picked up the grooming brush and triumphantly proclaimed, "I'm going to brush your hair."

Jake tried to fight her off, but his giggling left him ineffective. When they finally both collapsed, Jane became aware that the house was unusually quiet. She looked up and over the back of the sofa to the entranceway. Amy stood with her arms akimbo and her face scrunched into a disapproving glare.

Caroline and Thomas came from behind her, their faces still flushed from exertion and panting heavily. They grinned.

"We got to go," explained Tom. "Amy came to get us."

Jane stood and twitched her clothes in place. She put a hand to her ruffled curls and realized she must look absurd. How strange to feel foolish in the eyes of a thirteen year old. Would she ever be comfortable around Greg's eldest daughter? With as much grace as she could muster, she helped Caroline catch her over-excited puppy and secure the leash. She spoke calmly and with dignity as she said good-bye to her visitors. When the door closed on their departing figures, she rested her forehead against the cool wood.

"Father, I *played* with those children. I *played! Me!* And then, along came Amy. . . Lord, does Amy play? I'm a stuffy old grown-up. I'm set in my ways. What is happening? I don't think I've played since I was a very little child. Wasn't that wrong? Didn't I miss something? Isn't Amy missing that same something?"

fourteen

Jane pulled up in front of the large house and slowly withdrew her keys. She sat in the car wondering how she would be received. This was not Greg's parents, but Kathy's. How would they feel about another woman receiving attention from their son-in-law, their deceased daughter's husband?

Sending up a prayer that she wouldn't make a fool of herself, she opened the car door and came around to the sidewalk. The front door opened and Caroline, Tom, and Jake ran down the walkway to meet her. Their greeting gave Jane the courage she needed to step into the house.

"Grandma sent Daddy to get antacid. Gramps ate too much," Jake giggled. Clearly such a disaster was unknown to the boy.

An elegant woman in a flowing bronze caftan came to greet her. A subtle fragrance floated around her. She extended a well-manicured hand bedecked with jewels.

"Hello, I'm Cynthia Standish," she said.

"Jane Freedman." Jane put out her hand, hoping she showed the same confidence she exhibited when meeting a new client. The brief, cold handshake did not reassure her.

Uh-oh, thought Jane. *I'm under inspection.*

Cynthia Standish did covertly study the young woman as she took off her coat. Jane saw her relax a mite, and the tight polite smile spread to include her dark glittering eyes. Evidently, Greg's mother-in-law found the intruder to be less than comparable to her own daughter's beauty.

"Come," she said with warmth, "the children tell me you know little of our family."

Having spent hours in conversation with Caroline, Jake, and Tom over the past few months, Jane doubted that the children

91

would tell anyone that she "knew little of" any family. Jane recognized the polite statement as a conversational gambit designed to introduce the subject Mrs. Standish preferred. It soon became apparent that the topic of choice was Kathy Standish Boskell.

"I'm so sorry you never knew the children's mother. She radiated life. People actually came to a standstill as they admired her. Stunning, clever, gifted."

She fluttered a hand before her as if to say, "enough of that for now," and turned to address her grandchildren.

"Let's take Miss Freedman in to see the portraits, shall we, children? Austin is lying down at the moment," Mrs. Standish informed her guest, and her guest assumed that Austin must be Gramps.

With quick steps, Cynthia Standish led Jane to a room just off the main entrance. She flung back the double doors, touched the switch for lighting, and exposed Jane to the dazzling beauty of Greg's first wife. The exquisitely executed portraits hung on all four walls. Some were photographs and several were oil paintings.

The sheer elegance of the room demanded attention. Jane's intimate knowledge of interior design jumped into gear, and she analyzed the style and arrangement of the room. She judged it too ostentatious for her own taste, but nonetheless elegant. Countless portraits lined the walls as in a professional gallery, each with expert lighting to add to their distinction. Although many people were represented, it was the twins, Katherine and Kathleen, who took the limelight.

As Jane gazed at the pictures, she decided it didn't matter which one was which. Their beauty would have been unfair singly. In double force, it was enough to make a simple girl cut and run.

A smug smile settled on Cynthia Standish's face. She led Jane around the room with the air of the guide in a museum. She introduced the members of the family and gave a full account of each accomplishment the twins had achieved.

Jane comforted herself with the thought that these representations of the twins' astonishing beauty had been enhanced. Painters tended to flatter, and photographers had the airbrush technique to enhance natural beauty. Jane knew these two had bad hair days just like the rest of mortal women.

Mrs. Standish grew ever more animated as they progressed around the room. The children followed as well as Jane and obviously soaked in all the lore of their lost mother. Mrs. Standish told the stories with skill. She didn't ramble through the accounts but delivered her anecdotes as a dinner speaker, holding the listeners in the palm of her hand.

She loves her children, thought Jane. *It must have been very hard for her to lose Kathy. If she suspects that Greg's interested in me romantically, it's opening old wounds. I'll have to be tolerant of her glacial attitude toward me. It's probably masking her pain. Lord, help me to be wise and to sweeten my words and actions with Your love.*

No sooner had the words been formed in prayer than God sent reinforcements in the form of Greg.

"Here you are," he exclaimed from the doorway. He held a package in his hand and crossed to give it to his mother-in-law. "They had the brand you wanted at the first drugstore I tried." He smiled as he handed her the drugstore bag, and Jane felt he was also sending his mother-in-law another message. He turned to Jane before she had a chance to puzzle over the interchange.

"I see you found the house." His warm smile reached out to her, telling without words that he knew she'd been given a hard time, and now he'd stand beside her. She moved instinctively to his side where he took her hand.

Mrs. Standish turned away, holding the pharmacy bag in a clenched fist against her chest.

"This brand is the only one that really helps Austin with one of his upsets," she said. Her tone implied she would not appreciate an argument.

"It's fortunate that others must think so too," said Greg

agreeably. "It isn't nearly as hard to find as it used to be."

"The children are working a jigsaw puzzle," his mother-in-law said. "Perhaps you'd like to help, Miss Freedman."

"I've never done one," she admitted. That sent the children to clamoring their disbelief. It was unbelievable that a person could go through holidays without a jigsaw puzzle set up somewhere. They dragged her off to the living room where Gramps slept on the couch and Amy bent over the card table.

Mrs. Standish crossed to her husband and gently shook his shoulder to rouse him. She pushed the medicine into his hand.

"What, what?" he spoke in confusion. "Cynthia, I'm fine now. I told you this wasn't needed. I just needed a rest."

A low conversation ensued between the older couple.

The children rushed to Amy's side, leaving Greg and Jane in the doorway surveying the scene. Greg's arm settled around Jane's waist, and he gave her a reassuring squeeze. He bent to whisper in her ear.

"I knew it was a plot to get me out of the house, but I couldn't courteously refuse. She wanted to inspect you without interference." It was half apology and half explanation.

"I lived," Jane said. Then as an afterthought, she added, "Kathy was beautiful."

"Yes, she was," agreed Greg. "But look at her mother, Jane. In twenty years, Kathy would have had that same stiff, elegant, uncompromising cold beauty. Certain aspects of her personality mirrored her mother's. Kate may look the same, but she's cut out of a different cloth. I don't want you to think that I didn't love Kathy. I did. But sometimes it was hard."

He sighed as he watched his in-laws. Jane turned her attention to them and tried to identify what so bothered Greg. They continued to talk softly. But the positions of their bodies spoke volumes. Mrs. Standish was displeased and Mr. Standish was placating. Jane doubted whether the wife's irritation was truly over something the husband had done. Perhaps he was a convenient scapegoat for her petulance. Whatever the case, the situation looked extremely uncomfortable.

Greg squeezed her shoulders affectionately. "Kathy was just enough like her mother to be her favorite. Kate's more of a rebel. You'll like her."

Jake came rushing back to the door and took Jane by the hand. "Come try it," he demanded, dragging her toward the puzzle table. "I'll help you. I'm pretty good."

He pushed Jane into a seat beside Amy.

"Hello, Amy." Jane smiled at the teenager.

Amy started to rise, intent on leaving, but her father put a warning hand on her shoulder. Amy sunk back down and said, "Hello, Miss Freedman."

Jane caught an almost imperceptible squeeze by the father's hand on his uncooperative daughter's shoulder.

"I'm glad you could join us today," the daughter finished her greeting. Politely said, the greeting held as much warmth as Jane had received from the grandmother.

"Thank you, Amy." Jane searched for something else to say. "I astonished your brothers and sister by admitting I've never done a jigsaw puzzle. Is there a technique?"

Amy looked at her sharply as if to determine if she were being hoaxed.

"Well," she said reluctantly, "we've sorted out all the straight edge pieces first and done the border. Then these bowls have pieces sorted by color."

She reached across the table and selected a bowl to pass to Jane.

"This should be an easy one to start with. It's the water-wheel here in the picture." She pointed out the segment on the front of the box.

"I'll help," said Jake again. He nudged his father aside and half sat on the corner of Jane's chair. Greg laughed and took up another chair on the other side of Amy. They worked for almost an hour. Jane's helper left her after a few minutes, but Tom took his place and so the boys traded off assisting her. Caroline and her father put together a flock of geese. Amy worked on the stream of water. Mr. Standish came over to introduce himself and put a puzzle piece in but didn't stay.

"Gramps does that all the time," explained Amy, as if she'd forgotten that she was trying not to speak to Jane unless necessary. "We could finish the puzzle in nothing flat if he would just sit down and help us, but he doesn't." She wasn't angry, just explaining her grandfather's quirk. "He comes over about every thirty minutes or so, picks up a piece and sticks it in. Sometimes, it's the piece you've been looking for for ages. It's aggravating." She smiled, showing she loved the "aggravating" old man.

They took a break at five-thirty for coffee and pumpkin pie.

"Miss Freedman made a pumpkin pie," said Jake.

Jane gasped. She did *not* want the story of her pumpkin pie related to this audience.

"Don't you dare say one more word about that pie, Jacob Boskell," she commanded. "You remember in the Bible it says to think on things that are lovely, pure, of good repute, and excellent. There's no need to think on my lowly pie."

Tom and Jake laughed.

"Was the pie similar to one of Kate's creations?" asked Mr. Standish.

"It was lovely," defended Caroline.

"Hmm," said Gramps. "Covered with whipped cream, was it?"

They all laughed, and Jane blushed. She hoped the conversation would turn before one of the boys blurted out what had happened to that pie.

The door to the hall opened and Kate walked in. It had to be Kate. There was no mistaking that breathtaking beauty. So much for the theory of airbrushed photography or an artist's kind brush.

Kate beamed at the assembled group. Jane read love and goodwill in her expression.

I like her, she thought, surprised at herself.

fifteen

Amy jumped out of her chair, running to hug her aunt. She led her back to the card table with triumph in her eye. Jane almost expected her to announce "You see, Miss Freedman, you could never compete" in that exaggerated confidence she'd used at their first meeting at Mike's Midtown Burgers.

Instead, Amy introduced her without any fuss.

"I'm in love with Princess, Jane," said Kate with a twinkle in her eye. "I want a puppy out of Suggums' next litter."

Jane laughed, responding to the woman's casual friendliness. "That'll be at least eighteen months away. I won't breed her again this year."

Gramps gave his daughter a hug, but Mrs. Standish regarded her with a frown.

"I thought you were to be gone only an hour after dinner?"

Kate shrugged letting the reprimand roll off her back.

"I met some friends down at the art gallery and we went out for coffee," was all the explanation she offered.

Kate turned to Jane. "I hear you're involved with the new Mark Banner's Designs in Antiquity Showroom."

Jane nodded. "I'm the district manager. Our grand opening is tomorrow. Timed for the 'Annual Biggest Shopping Day of the Year.' "

Kate took Amy's chair. "I'd like you to look at some paintings I've been experimenting with. It's the old impressionists' style. It's caught my attention, and I've had fun reproducing the era." She smiled in a friendly way and turned toward Greg. "I don't know how much my brother-in-law has told you. He's not really into art. I don't stay long with any one thing. I drive my agent crazy, but most of it sells so I don't worry. I'm hardly the starving artist." She waved her hand to

97

indicate her parents' opulent home. "I'll never be a van Gogh, or even Picasso, because I have too much fun. For me it's all the creative process."

Another person speaking these words might have sounded pretentious and phony, but not Kate with her clear, direct gaze. Her pleasant smile reassured and her warm voice resonated sincerity.

"I'd be glad to look at your paintings," answered Jane. "Were you looking for a market?"

Kate frowned, tiny little creases running across her high brow and in no way marring that look of exquisite beauty. "No, not really." She giggled. "I was thinking that should you ever need a particular artwork commissioned I might be able to help you out."

Of course, thought Jane, but still could not be offended. *She offered to do me a favor. I took it as she needed a favor.*

"Let me help with the puzzle," offered Kate, and they regrouped around the table.

A glowing Amy sat down next to her aunt Kate, and Jane observed the similarity of their clothing. Remembering her first encounter with Greg's daughter, Jane envisioned Amy in trendy teen threads. She took a second look as she realized that Amy wore a loose tunic top like her aunt's with beads dangling around her neck. Both wore broomstick skirts in dark yet vibrant colors.

Mr. Standish must have noticed the same thing.

"Did you two go shopping together?" he asked.

"Hum?" Kate cocked an eyebrow at her father.

"You and Amy," he explained. "Your outfits."

Kate turned to scrutinize her niece and Amy blushed. Jane felt uncomfortable recognizing the young girl's embarrassment. Kate recognized the same discomfort and gave her niece a quick hardy hug.

"Hey! Imitation is the sincerest form of flattery," she laughed and threw a warning glance at her mother. The look was ignored.

"I think a child should dress like a child," said Grand-mother Standish. "Of course this is an improvement over drooping denim and blue nail polish." An uncomfortable tension stilled the atmosphere in the room as she continued, oblivious to the reaction of her family. "Kate, you never did dress with the elegance that Kathy had, and it would be preferable if she were still here to guide her daughter as she develops her taste." She smiled at her granddaughter, a heavy, condescending smile. "I'd be glad to take you shopping, Dear, if you're showing a genuine interest in style."

"Mother, I *chose*," said Kate, emphasizing the last word. Her own smile remained tightly on her lips, but the words sounded cold and her eyes flashed with anger. "I *chose* to be different from my sister. Everyone has the right to be their own person."

"Well, of course, Dear." A puzzled frown flitted across the older woman's face.

"There wasn't any 'of course' about it," said Kate with a brittle edge in her tone.

"Ahem." Mr. Standish cleared his throat pointedly, attracting his daughter's eye. He cast her a frown and a minuscule shake of his head.

Kate visibly relaxed and seemed to shake loose a personal demon. "Ah well, Mother. I did it for you."

She laughed softly even as her mother's posture grew rigid against some expected onslaught.

"You had a terrible time telling us apart," Kate continued, carefully studying the jigsaw puzzle piece she had in her hand. "I was the tacky one. It made it easier once I started choosing my own duds."

Mrs. Standish shrugged her shoulders in an elegant gesture and turned to walk away from the circle.

Kate held her puzzle piece aloft and shook it in the air.

"I just saw where this piece belonged a minute ago. Now where was that? How aggravating! Help me find it, kids. It looks like there's a goose eye here on the little nubby piece sticking out."

The boys giggled and Caroline grabbed the box top to look at the picture. The uncomfortable moment passed.

When the dessert and coffee came in on an elegant cherry tea cart, Kate moved over to serve with the children following her. Jane sat alone at the puzzle table with Amy. Caroline and Jacob carefully carried the china plates with a slice of pie over to serve them. Caroline skipped back to get her own piece and Jake followed.

"You like her, don't you?" asked Amy.

"Caroline?" Jane smiled as she watched the little girl argue with Jacob over who got the next piece.

"Aunt Kate."

Jane shifted her gaze to the graceful woman laughing at something Mr. Standish said while she poured the coffee from an ornate silver pot.

"Yes, I like her. She seems. . . ," she paused, searching for the right word, "personable."

"Dad loves her. If he can't marry her, it's because he can't marry anyone. He's devastated by my mother's death. It shook the foundation of his soul."

The depth of feeling expressed in the last utterance riveted Jane's full attention on Amy. The teen sat in her exaggerated stiff posture, her back ramrod straight. She blinked behind the glasses. The somber green eyes idolized her aunt. The studied mournfulness in Amy's words tempted Jane to dismiss the melodrama as hokey. She immediately thought, *Oh, come on, lighten up a bit, Kid.*

Gazing at the intent look on Amy's face, Jane bit her lower lip. This child was too complex for Jane's comfort. The boys were boisterous. Caroline was exuberant. Amy was pensive and troubled and unpredictable.

The boys, when they deigned to visit Jane after school, talked openly. They said they came to help Caroline with Suggums and her brood. Caroline would change the paper in the pen, wash out the water dish, and carry the puppies outside to run. The boys greeted the dogs and cornered Jane as someone who would listen to them.

Jane *always* listened to them attentively. She marveled at their personalities. She'd never thought that these shorter people who populated the earth in droves called the next generation possessed individual minds. In spite of herself, she recognized their uniqueness.

She laughed at their jokes. She did not laugh at their grand ideas of getting big dogs when they were older. She sympathized with their plight regarding the school P.E. coach who seemed ill-suited for his job. One day the boys brought over a video and a bag of microwave popcorn, wanting to share one of their favorite cartoons with their friend.

That time Caroline had stewed in a put-upon attitude. The boys encroached on her friendship with Suggums' owner. Even as her lower lip stuck out in a pout, she tolerated their intrusion. After all, many times the boys had better things to do than hang with their older sister.

All in all, Jane had enjoyed the camaraderie of the three youngest Boskells. She didn't have answers to all their questions. She sometimes had to exert some authority to curb their excessive energy. But their behavior never stumped her. Their behavior never made her feel uneasy, nervous, or apprehensive. What was it about Amy that made Jane so wary?

She looked again at Amy's clothes modeled after her aunt. She saw the stilted attitude, the intent concentration on the too serious face, and a young reflection of her grandmother.

She makes me nervous because she doesn't add up. I don't know what she'll do or say next. She's an unpleasant surprise about to come unwrapped in my presence. Greg needs to take her to a counselor of some kind. If I tell him that, he's going to think I'm the one off my rocker. What do I know about adolescents? I think I may have even skipped the stage myself.

"Someday they'll recognize that the friendship they have is based on a deep abiding love." Amy turned to Jane and smiled. "Do you know they never fight?" She shook her head ever so slightly and repeated the word in a whisper. "Never."

"You know, Amy," Jane said, "people have a tendency to think and feel in ways that are entirely different from what we expect. People don't always see the things that we might think are obvious. And sometimes the assumptions we make about other people are wrong."

Amy nodded enthusiastically as if Jane had suddenly agreed with her. "That's just why I had to speak to you. I knew that since you're a stranger, you couldn't see. You're an outsider so you couldn't be expected to realize what the family has known for a long time. But, I'm glad you came today. Now that you've seen Dad and Aunt Kate together, I know you can see for yourself how it is. One day they'll get married."

That wasn't at all what Jane had tried to get across. Amy's misinterpretation silenced any further attempts to communicate.

"You're leaving?" Mrs. Standish's voice rose in disapproval. She sat rigidly on the sofa beside her husband, her eyes pinning her daughter with disapproval. "Thanksgiving is a holiday for family," she continued in a voice meant to lecture. "Families gather for the holiday to celebrate their connection. I expect you to put aside outside engagements for a more suitable time. This is a time to spend with us."

"Mother," Kate began with a voice full of reason, "I live with you so I see you every day. I work at Greg's house so I see that part of the family most days. It isn't as if I've flown in from New York to visit for the weekend."

"Sarcasm." Mrs. Standish turned an eye to her husband. He shrugged as if to say it was her war and he wasn't enlisting for the battle.

"Very well, Kate." Her mother smoothed a nonexistent wrinkle on the material of her skirt as it lay across her knee. "Bid our guest good-bye. At least in that way you can be a good example for your nieces and nephews."

Kate bounced up and came across to where Jane still sat with Amy. Her eyebrows arched and a merry smile tipped up the corners of her mouth. She did not look chastened.

"I'm glad we met, Jane. See you around, Amy. We'll go

Christmas shopping sometime in the next couple of weeks." She pirouetted with grace, waved carelessly at the boys and Greg, gave a quick squeeze hug to her dad and Caroline, and flitted out of the room.

Amy sighed. Jane looked over at the young girl's face and wondered what kind of convoluted thinking went on behind that satisfied expression.

That old idea of "This isn't any of my business" sure sounds good right now.

Lord, what do You want me to do here? I'm feeling very nervous about this whole thing. Should I tell Greg the kind of things Amy talks about? I've never even told him about that lunch a year ago. Shouldn't he be doing something about Amy's fantasies? So many people could get hurt here. Father, I don't want to be one of them. But I really care about this family. Ohh, I'm totally unprepared for this kind of thing. Get me out of this!

sixteen

Jane impatiently tapped her fingers on the big steering wheel of the company van. The light turned green for the third time and she inched her way toward the intersection. Holiday traffic in Denver normally clogged the streets, but just two blocks from the mall, it had jelled into a glutinous mass that threatened to stick solid. The drizzling rain, the early dusk, the quickly dropping temperature, and a fender bender in the intersection further complicated matters. Jane figured she wouldn't get this cargo to the unloading dock until late evening.

Her stomach growled. She glanced at the digital clock on the dash—6:14. She'd left the store a little after nine that morning. No wonder her stomach protested. The light changed again and she crept forward all of two yards. The soft chiming ring of the company cell phone caught her attention. She reached over to the passenger seat and plucked the instrument out of her purse.

"Hi, Jane," Mark's cheerful voice came through. Mark Banner had been with them the last month but was due to go back East and home for Christmas. He thrived on the hurly-burly activity surrounding the Grand Opening and, true to form, enjoyed the two weeks of last-minute preparation of the gallery and showroom. He'd also driven everyone nuts with his rendition of "there's no place like home for the holidays." The boss was both a pleasure to be around and a pain in the neck. "Bunny tells me you're stuck in traffic."

"Yep," she answered. "You could send some burly men down the street. They could carry the merchandise piece by piece and get it there quicker than I'm going to be able to."

"Don't think we're that desperate," he chuckled. "Bunny also said you had some trouble with the paperwork."

"Yes, I was hung up for over two hours because the B-23 form was missing. I had our copy, but the copy attached to the order was not."

"Not?"

"Not attached."

"Sorry you ran into such a snag, but I'm glad you went to the airport. Anyone with less authority would still be sitting there."

Jane nodded. "I put a call through to the Maryland office and they faxed out the forms." Mark was right. She had made a few phone calls to the right people and authorized duplicates where needed. Someone else would have had to locate Mark or herself before the ball could have started rolling again. That's why she picked up airfreighted merchandise.

"You missed a record day here at the gallery," Mark gloated. The man reveled in the excitement of brisk business.

"Mark, when you've only been open twelve days," she pointed out in a halfhearted attempt to burst his bubble, "it's pretty easy to break your previous records."

His friendly, natural laugh made it hard to remember he drove an Italian sports car, wore a watch that cost more than all of her kitchen appliances, and special ordered his shoes. Jane felt a torrent of tension ease out of her shoulders. His manner often had that effect on her. She appreciated him. Mark Banner didn't lead the designer industry. He hopped, skipped, and jumped ahead of it, and the rest of the trade struggled just to keep their collective eye on him and follow.

"Well, I just wanted to touch base with you before I head back East. I have a flight out in an hour. It's home for the holidays for me. Susan will have homemade pumpkin pie and wassail." Susan was his five-year-old daughter, and for an instant the pumpkin pie smeared across her floor came back to haunt Jane. She wondered if his little girl was a better cook than she was. She changed her line of thought.

"Don't come out the north entrance or you won't make your flight." Jane took her gloved hand and wiped some of the moisture off the inside of the windshield. Red taillights declared the jammed roadway still impassable.

"Greg Boskell came by with his kids," said Mark.

"Oh?" With one hand, Jane pulled her knit scarf tighter around her neck and tugged at the fuzzy hat that kept her ears warm. The heater on the van had not held out against the cold of the winter storm. Raindrops pinged against the windshield signaling the change from shower to sleet.

"He said he hasn't seen you since Thanksgiving, and I must be a slave driver."

"Thanksgiving was only two weeks ago. We, meaning you, me, and the staff have all been busy, Mark. I've talked to him on the phone and I think he understands. You're probably reading more into it than there is."

"It was the mournful expression of a little girl with a bush of dark blond locks for hair. She's the one who made me feel like you had deserted the family."

Jane smiled as an image of Caroline came to her mind. Her fine curly hair did tend to stand on end when she removed a knit hat she'd been wearing against the cold. Talk about a bad hair day. You could almost hear Caroline's light brown hair SPROING! when she pulled off her headgear.

"That was Caroline. She has one of Suggums' puppies."

"So she said. I've got to run, Jane. My last official communiqué to my assistant is to remember the 'reason for the season' as they say. You know I don't approve of my employees being workaholics to the detriment of their families."

"I don't have a family, remember?" Jane shot back. How irritating that Mark was trying to make something significant out of a friend dropping by the store.

I did tell Greg I loved him. And I do. Are there depths of love? I'm already uncomfortable in the shallow end of the pool, and Mark wants me to jump off the high board into the deep end.

"Maybe not, but you have a fan club now, and you mustn't neglect your public."

"Very funny. Have a nice trip. Season's greetings to your daughter. Hug her tight for me."

"I hear you, Jane. What you're really saying is get out of your life and get back to my own."

"If the shoe fits. . ."

"Love you too." Mark laughed, and then said in his best Humphrey Bogart voice, "Merry Christmas, Sweetheart. I'll be seeing you, Kid."

"Yeah, yeah. Merry Christmas and good-bye." Jane flipped the phone closed and stuck it in her bag. One more light change and she should be through the clogged intersection.

Why does Mark's pushy badgering make me relax and Greg's gentle voice and Mickey Mouse smile make me neurotic? This is confusing and uncomfortable and I'm not sure making a commitment is worth the upheaval.

She wasn't good at family things, and ever since the Thanksgiving evening at the Standish home, Jane had avoided Greg. Sure she was busy, but that wasn't really it. She didn't lie to herself. Didn't she make extra efforts to get by the house to spend an odd hour with Suggums, or even take her to the showroom where she sat like a little lady in one of the displays as if she were stuffed and exhibited? If she could squeeze in time to see her dog and bend a few rules so the dog wouldn't be lonely, couldn't she do the same for the man who had declared his love and wrung a like confession out of her? Apparently not.

Finally she nosed the big van into the covered unloading bay.

Our ritzy merchandise won't get damaged by exposure to the elements. But what about my heart? Is my heart going to get damaged by exposure to the real world? What a basket case I have become, she chastised herself as she left the men from the store unloading the furniture. *I try my best to put the whole situation out of my mind and a cold, stark loading dock reminds me of Greg's love and friendship. It's a good thing the opening has demanded all of my attention or wonderful, warm, and desirable Greg Boskell would have gotten the cold shoulder. I'm just not good at this family thing.*

I think I said that before.

Well, I'm not!

A phrase from her musing jumped back at her. "Real world."

What baloney, she thought. *I was forced into the real world when I packed my bag and left home.*

Forty-five minutes later, Jane walked into the store office with her arms loaded. Bunny jumped to help her with as much vitality as Suggums who came out of her office basket with a bound and a bark of greeting.

"How's it going?" Jane asked her coworker as she sunk into the chair, bent over, and scooped Suggums into her lap. "How's my little girl?" she asked the dog while rubbing her sides and back. "Was she any trouble?"

"Are you asking the dog if I was any trouble?" quizzed Bunny. "No, I don't think I was. If you're asking me if Suggums was any trouble, the answer is no. I walked her in cold, bitter wind and gave her half of my sub sandwich. She seemed content enough."

"I never expected to be gone so long. Thanks."

"Don't mention it," Bunny said. "You missed Mark. He did his Fred Astaire imitation of Bing Crosby's 'White Christmas.' "

"He was tap dancing for the customers." Jane had been around Mark long enough to know his shenanigans. She rolled her eyes heavenward.

Bunny giggled. "And singing. He couldn't help himself. The song was playing on the mall PA system and there was a group of five or six kids. The music, the audience—you know the boss."

"And did the crowd grow?"

"Yes."

"And did he pick one little girl out to be his Ginger Rogers?"

"Yes."

"Bunny, there's one great thing about being in Denver this Christmas."

"That is. . . ?"

"The Christmas office party in Maryland."

"He might fly back to join us," Bunny warned.

"I didn't tell him when ours was scheduled, did you?"

Bunny shook her head. They looked at each other with mock seriousness and then burst into laughter.

"A nice young man with a herd of children came by looking for you," Bunny said.

Greg, again. To Bunny, anyone under forty was young; anyone patient enough to shop with kids was nice.

Jane knew Greg was a "nice young man." Wasn't her whole emotional state in turmoil because of him? Didn't she want to rush into his arms one minute and hide from him the next? Didn't she pray for the courage to commit to this "nice young man"? Didn't she pray the Lord would remove her heart so it wouldn't yearn so for the "nice young man"? Hadn't she said a dozen times, "I don't know what I want, Father, please tell me what I want"?

Jane held up a hand to ward off the matchmaking she felt coming. "Don't you start on me too, Bunny."

"Too?"

"Don't play innocent. Mark's already given me his two cents' worth, and I don't need yours."

Jane sorted the freight paperwork and turned her chair to address the computer. She needed to log in the entries. Bunny raised her eyebrows but refrained from making a comment. Jane pretended not to notice.

The phone rang and Bunny picked up the receiver. After a brief interchange she hung up to relay the message.

"Jennifer on the floor says someone's in the gallery asking for you. I said you'd be right down. I'll do the entries for you."

Jane put a brake on the emotions as they came flooding to the surface. She turned to the older woman, making an all-out effort to control her face and hoping not to expose her thoughts. With narrowed eyes and lips pressed in a firm line, Jane nodded her assent.

It was Greg and his family for sure. Bunny knew it was and had deliberately manipulated the situation so she'd have to go down. Bunny wanted her to date Greg. Mark wanted her to date Greg. Greg wanted her to date Greg. She even wanted her to date Greg.

Dear Lord, do You want me to date Greg? Do You want me to marry him? Do You want me to help Amy, or do You just want me to get out of the way so someone more capable can do it?

"You stay here," she snapped.

"Was that addressed to you or to me?" Bunny asked the dog.

Jane marched out of the office and turned down the corridor to the steps leading to the public area of the gallery. She'd be friendly, especially to Caroline, who didn't deserve to be treated shabbily by her new friend. But as soon as the holidays were over and things settled down, she was going to have a talk with Greg.

Yes, Greg, I love you as a good friend, but I don't see any future in our becoming more involved.

She entered the showroom. Not Greg and family but Kate waited for her.

"Hi," said Kate. "This place is fabulous. I love the lighting on the Oriental displays. And the Egyptian motif in the bedroom almost makes me want to finally establish a home of my own and give myself over to a spree of decorating."

"Hi, Kate," Jane answered. Relief mixed with disappointment. She wanted to see Greg, talk to him without a phone line between them, maybe share one more kiss before she told him the situation was impossible. *I'm a real wuss,* she thought, but she smiled a warm greeting for Kate.

"We're shopping, my friend and I," explained her visitor. "We had to separate to get the things we'd picked out for each other. His name is Dave. He's a stock broker. Doesn't that sound stuffy?" Her nose wrinkled and her eyes gleamed. "But he's very special. I've tried to hold his profession against him and failed."

Jane wanted to know how special but didn't think she had the right to just outright ask.

"I know what he's going to get me," said Kate. "He's not at all subtle. I knew when he picked it out. His eyes lit up, and he couldn't keep them from roaming back to it. Then almost immediately he tells me it's time to go our own way for awhile and then tells me which store to stay out of. No James Bond intrigue, more like clear glass subterfuge."

Jane laughed. "I'm glad you came to the gallery. Are you going to look for something for Dave here?"

"No, I came to see you." Kate tilted her head and openly examined Jane. "You are a nice person. Caroline and the boys are smitten. That's an old-fashioned word, isn't it? But it fits. They would adopt you."

"I think a lot of them too."

"Very properly said, Miss Freedman." Kate nodded primly, then let out a nimble peal of laughter, reminding Jane of wind chimes, not the heavy clanking ones, but thin hollow metal tubes bouncing lightly off each other in the slightest breeze. "They're here, you know,"

"Greg and the kids?" When she saw Kate waiting for her in the showroom, Jane assumed the family must have gone home hours before. It was one of those nebulous thoughts to protect oneself. *Of course, they've gone home. Be still, my heart.* That kind of psychological hippity-hop used to deny her disappointment.

Kate nodded. "They're ice-skating. Come on out to the rail, and let's see if we can spot them."

Jane followed Kate out the front of the store, and they dodged shoppers to get to the rail encircling the center of the mall. Two stories below, figures of all sizes and abilities crowded the skating rink, gliding across the ice.

After a few moments, Kate pointed. "There are the little guys. And Greg and Amy are about three yards ahead of them. It amazes me that the kids skate so well. I guess when they start young it's easier."

Jane watched Greg and Amy. They skated in tandem with their arms crossed before them and hands held. He spoke to her and she laughed up at him. She looked content and happy as a teenager should. She was beside her dad and had a firm grip on him.

That's how it should be, thought Jane. *She needs him to be her father. All of him. This is what he should be concentrating on at this time.*

Is this an answer to my prayer? Is God showing me that I'm a disruptive force to this family?

Kate waved enthusiastically and at first Jane thought she was trying to attract the skaters' attention. Kate grasped Jane's arm and gave her an excited shake as she turned her toward the stream of shoppers.

"Here comes Dave. See the bag from Balmore's gripped in his hand? It's the most gorgeous lush blue sweater you ever saw."

Kate waved until she attracted a man's attention. As soon as he reached her side, Kate put her arms around his waist and gave him a bear hug.

Dave's short, solidly built frame bulged in the sweatshirt he wore under a suede leather jacket. His hair sat in tight dark curls all over his head. Black bushy eyebrows peeked over the dark rims of thick glasses. Blue eyes sparkled with good cheer.

"Only one package?" she asked with disappointment.

"If you must know, I took some out to the car and put them in the trunk so you wouldn't see."

Kate cocked an eyebrow at him. "Are you telling me you're more devious than I've been led to believe?"

"I'm telling you that after a year of dating you, I've acquired a devious nature." He grinned impishly at her and tightened his hug. "What can I say? You're good for me."

Kate gave an exaggerated pout and turned to Jane.

"Jane, this is the love of my life, Dave Brandt. Dave, this is Jane whose fame is either her dog who had marvelous puppies or her way with pumpkin pie, depending on which member of my family you talk to."

"Who's been talking about that pie?" demanded Jane, grinning in spite of herself.

"I'm not telling."

"Well, I was told to fix my pie in the same manner as a certain aunt."

"I admit to covering disastrous baked goods with whipped cream, but I never covered anyone's face with the baked goods." A sly smile tugged at her features, and Kate had a knowing look in her eye.

"Oh, you heard the *whole* story."

"I confess," said Dave. "I heard the story from Kate. You could buy my silence at an exorbitant price, but I believe the little Boskells are like town criers, and you'd be wasting your money."

Jane groaned and covered her eyes with one hand. She shook her head acknowledging defeat. There was nothing to do but live down the incident. Surprised, she realized she enjoyed this couple's mild teasing. A thought of Amy disturbed her.

"Are you acquainted with the Boskell children?" she asked Dave.

"I was Jake's and Tom's soccer coach. I met Caroline once when Greg picked them up after practice. Then Kate came to pick them up. From thenceforth, the lovely aunt took on the job of transporting the boys to and from soccer."

"Pretty full of yourself, aren't you?" badgered Kate with a grin of approval. Clearly, she admired this sturdy fellow with thick glasses and bushy eyebrows. He waggled those eyebrows at her and she laughed.

"Babe, as much as I'd like to buy out the stores for you tonight, the roads are turning into long, intersecting ice rinks even as we speak."

"Getting bad out there?" Kate frowned.

"We need to inch our way home." He turned to Jane, and extended his hand. "It was nice to meet you. Perhaps Kate,

Greg, you, and I can eat out and catch a movie. *After* the New Year. I think everybody is suffering from social calendar overload now."

Jane nodded her agreement and said good-bye. She watched them weave their way toward the escalator before going back into the gallery. They looked like a couple. They looked happy.

I wonder if Amy knows of her aunt's romantic interest.

"Jane," a familiar voice stopped her as she passed the living room display done in sable browns and muted reds. A flutter in her midsection signaled her heart to skip a beat, and she turned with a welcome lifting the corners of her mouth in a smile.

Jane looked into Greg's eyes and forgot all the problems her mind so easily created when she stewed over their relationship. She forgot it was nine days 'til Christmas and the gallery was doing record business. She forgot she was an executive. She forgot she was at work. She walked into his arms, held him close to her, and rested her weary head against his chest.

seventeen

"Now if we could get a chance to do this every day, I could be a happy man." Greg rested his chin on top of her head.

"I've been avoiding you," Jane confessed.

"No kidding?"

"Well, you said you love me." Her tone was accusatory.

"Well, you said you love me." His tone was more congenial.

"I do," she admitted. "I just don't think I'm going to be very good at it."

"Number one, you think too much. Number two, let me be the judge of whether you're good at it or not. Number three, so far you've knocked my socks off, so you can't be all that bad."

"Your socks are on."

"It's an expression."

"It doesn't make sense."

"Do you want me to kiss you right here in your showroom?"

"No!"

"Quit spouting drivel, or I'll be forced to cover the fount."

Greg felt her shoulders shake and he tilted her head back with one hand to look at her face. She laughed up at him and he grinned as he planted a swift kiss on her smiling lips.

"Let me take you home tonight."

"What?" The request jerked Jane back to the here and now.

"Take you home. The kids and I will wait for you."

"Why?"

"Because from what I hear, there is a glacier forming on the parking lot. I saw you standing next to Kate and Dave and hurried to turn in my skates. While I put on my shoes, I got the lowdown from other shoppers making haste to truck on home. I'd feel better if we escorted you to your front door."

"I've driven on snow and ice," Jane answered. "Colorado

doesn't have an exclusive on winter weather. Maryland can be fierce too."

"Why don't you just relax and let me do this for you?" Greg's low voice was persuasive. "It'll make me feel good."

"I've got Suggums with me."

"I'm not supposed to have room for her, or what? She's going to take up the whole backseat, and I'll have to leave a couple of my kids at the mall?"

"No." Jane's eyes twinkled at his silliness. "I meant yes, I will come, but there's Suggums as well as me to transport."

"Good, I thought about leaving the boys, but the nighttime security probably isn't up to dealing with their shenanigans. How soon can you be ready?"

"Since I started work at eight, I think I can leave now. I'll go back to the office, tell Bunny, and collect Suggums."

"Good." Greg reluctantly released her. "Meet me in the food court by the skate entrance."

"Yes, Sir."

Jane watched him leave. Nobody had ever made her feel the way he did. She gathered a great lung full of the holiday atmosphere in the mall and expelled it in a slow relaxing sigh.

Lord, all that stuff I've been telling You lately about getting me out of this situation—I've changed my mind. I want to stay. Now, I guess I should acknowledge that I need Your help. I don't want to botch this, not with Greg, not with Caroline, not with the boys, and not with Amy. Give to me what each one of them needs whether it be compassion, a listening ear, words of wisdom, whatever. Guide my tongue, let me be a blessing to each member of this family.

❧

The dash to the minivan demonstrated how slick the roads were to be. Greg held firmly to Jane's elbow and to Caroline's hand. Amy had both boys by the hand. Even in boots with good tread, the ice challenged each step.

"Dad, tell the boys to quit sliding on purpose," Amy called.

"Jacob, Thomas," he barked. "You've had enough ice-skating for one day. Just get to the car without being hurt."

"Are you going to put the chains on, Dad?" asked Tom.

"Yes."

"Can I help?" the boys chorused.

Greg chuckled. "Sure."

Inside the van, Caroline confiscated Suggums and wrapped her in an afghan kept in the back to keep the passengers warm. Greg put Jane in the passenger side of the front seat. Amy passed her another afghan.

"These are nice," Jane commented.

"We take them to Mile-High Stadium to watch the Broncos," said Caroline. "Suggums is shivering."

"Put her body next to yours and then cover both of you up with the blanket," suggested Jane.

"Here, let me help," said Amy. Amy unzipped Caroline's coat and gently tucked Suggums in under one of the folds. She then tucked the afghan around both her sister and the dog.

"I hope Princess is all right," moaned Caroline.

"She's fine, Caro; Betsy'll take good care of her." Amy turned to explain to Jane. "We left the puppy with our next door neighbor for the day. We knew we'd be gone for too many hours."

"Do you like the puppy, Amy?" Jane asked.

"Oh, yes!" Amy smiled. Jane felt warmed by the first genuine smile received from the teenager. "I asked Dad to get me a male for my birthday so we can breed puppies."

Amy's plan surprised Jane. The older sister had never visited nor shown an interest in all the weeks that the younger Boskell children had haunted Jane's house.

"When's your birthday?"

"The Saturday before Christmas."

Jane made a quick calculation. "You'll be fifteen then."

"Fourteen," admitted Amy.

"Grandma says she's really going to be twenty-one," put in Caroline.

A puzzled frown etched Jane's forehead. "I thought when we met last year, you were thirteen."

A blush colored Amy's cheeks and her eyes dimmed with embarrassment. "I was going to be thirteen in a few months." She grinned sheepishly and looked Jane in the eye with a glimmer of mischief that was startlingly reminiscent of her father's expression. "Close enough to count."

The driver's door jerked open.

"We've got the chains laid out. Now we're just going to roll onto them." Greg announced as he started the engine. He leaned out the open door. "Stand clear, boys!" he ordered, shifted gears, and eased the van back a few feet. He switched off the engine and hopped out of the car again.

"We'll get you home all right, Miss Freedman," said Caroline. "Daddy's good at this."

In a few minutes they were on their way. Even with four-wheel drive and chains, the short trip was hazardous.

Jane prayed not only for safety for those in their van but for the vehicles around. Several times the females in the car scrunched down in their seats and screwed their eyes shut in anticipation of being hit while one or the other of the boys hollered, "Wow! Look at that car slide!"

"I move for not taking the freeway home," said Greg.

"I second it," Jane agreed.

The car's heater began to warm up the interior of the minivan. Jane squirmed a little under her seat belt so she could angle her body in a more comfortable position to watch Greg as he drove and occasionally look to the backseat and speak with the children. Greg's strong hands capably gripped the steering wheel. His gloves strained over the knuckles. He really had big hands, but Jane knew them to be gentle. He proceeded cautiously, praying out loud when some-one started to skid near them.

"What a mess!" he said more than once.

Jane relaxed. Greg would get them home safely.

They turned into Jane's street next to the park. A trip that usually took fifteen minutes had taken them an hour.

"Dad, look!" exclaimed Jake.

"Yeah, I see it," Greg answered.

Just beyond Jane's house, a fire engine blocked the street. Greg pulled into Jane's driveway and switched off the engine.

"Wait here while I find out what's going on," he ordered.

"I want to go," begged Jake.

"Me too," said Tom.

"No, I'll be back in a jiff."

The door slammed shut. Greg hiked his coat collar around his neck as he took off down the street. Cold air rushed in with him when he returned and jumped once more into the driver's seat.

"The little creek bed bridge collapsed."

"Cool," said Tom. "Let's go look."

"Tom," growled his father, "it's no picnic out there. I fell twice. There aren't *patches* of ice. It's *all* ice without patches of pavement. Even the grass is coated with ice."

Tom knew there would be no excursions to the fascinating crumpled bridge tonight. Jane had to turn away to hide the grin that came to her face. Tom's expression clearly stated grown-ups just didn't know when a good opportunity knocked.

"Are we going to drive the long way home?" asked Amy.

"It's going to have to be the long, long way round," answered Greg. "Hitch Road has a tree down."

"They must be freezing," said Jane. "Should I make them some hot coffee?"

"They had a thermos from one of your neighbors."

"How long will it take us to get home, Daddy?" asked Caroline. "Princess will be crying for me."

"Princess is just fine, Caro," Greg's words echoed Amy's earlier reassurance. "Betsy will cuddle her if she cries."

"How long, Dad?" asked Amy.

"An hour or more," he answered.

Jane looked at the snow coming down now in big wet flakes to cover the ice already formed on everything in sight.

"I think the weather's getting worse," she said. "Why don't you camp in my living room and go home tomorrow?"

"Yeah!" said the boys, bouncing in their seats.

"Princess," wailed Caroline.

"You can call Betsy when we get in the house," said Greg.

"You'll stay?" Jane asked.

Greg nodded. He reached over and took her mittened hand in his gloved one. Even through the layers of cloth, the warming buzz of electricity connected between them. The comfort of looking into his face, seeing the affection in his smile and the underlying passion in his eyes sent a tremor down Jane's spine.

"You're cold," said Greg, noting the shiver.

Jane winked. "That shiver had nothing to do with cold. It's a good thing we're going to have a lot of chaperones, or you'd have to put on snowshoes and risk frostbite."

"You'd send me out in the cold."

"Well, at least call the neighbors and see if I could find you other accommodations."

"Then it's a good thing our Heavenly Father has provided us with little guardian angels."

They'd been speaking low enough that their words did not carry to the back of the car. Jake had unbuckled and wiggled his way to the front in time to catch the last lines.

"Who's an angel?" he asked.

Greg caught him and flipped him upside down over the console. "Not you, Buddy." He gave Jake a gentle shake and flipped him back to the rear.

"Come on, gang, we're invading an alien planet."

Thomas whooped and reached for the sliding door.

"I'm an alien?" Jane laughed.

"You're the earthling. We're the Martians." Kids piled out the side door. Greg took advantage of their preoccupation and stole a kiss from Jane. "Warning. Warning, Jane Freedman," he said in a robot voice. "The Martians have landed."

"Come on, Daddy!" An impatient voice moved them out of the car.

eighteen

"No peanut butter?" Incredulous, Tom wagged his head back and forth as he stood beside his hostess.

Jane sorted through the contents of her cabinets, trying to find something to feed her alien visitors. It seemed she didn't have the right food for feeding creatures from outer space.

"I've got bread and boysenberry jam," she offered.

"The bread has weeds in it," Tom pointed out with an ungracious snort. He looked at her multigrain loaf as if it truly were alien food.

"Boysenberry, poisonberry." Jacob gave an expressive shrug. What could you expect from a lady who only had one color of towels in her bathroom and a nightlight with flowers to boot?

"Have you got hot dogs?" asked Tom.

"No," Jane admitted. "No hot dogs."

Tom and Jake exchanged a look that spoke volumes.

"Tuna fish?" asked Tom.

Jane just shook her head.

Greg came into the kitchen to investigate why the dinner committee made groaning noises audible in the living room.

"Out, you're fired," he ordered the boys.

"Why?" asked Jake with a martyred look. "We're hungry. She needs us, Daddy. She hasn't a clue what's good."

Jane turned away from the earnest expression on the boy's face. She was between laughing at their antics and crying over her inability to provide a quick, spontaneous meal. Maybe she'd better rethink her decision to willingly join this family.

No, I've already made that decision a hundred times. Will I accept Greg's love along with a ready-made family, or will

I keep myself isolated and miss all the pleasure of being in love? Last vote, I had decided on taking the plunge, and I'm going to stick with my last choice. I'm tough. I can do this.

The boys left. Greg approached her from the back, wrapped his arms around her, and nuzzled her neck.

"Got any bouillon cubes?" he asked in the throaty low voice that made her toes tingle.

"Yes."

"Vegetables? Frozen? Canned? Anything?" He turned her in his arms to face him.

"Yes."

"Get out the biggest pot you have and let's get cooking." He kissed her softly across her forehead and started down, past the eyes, across the cheek, heading for her mouth.

"What are the kids doing?" she asked.

"They found a deck of cards and Amy's playing Whupya with them." He lightly touched her lips with his.

"I don't think I know the game." The words came out on a breath of air.

"Oh, but you're learning. You're getting the hang of it real well."

"Greg!" Jane squeaked just as he came in for another more intense kiss. He backed away.

"What?"

"Vegetables. Hungry children." He flustered her. This was too much emotion.

He moaned and collapsed against her, molding his body to hers and pulling her closer still within his arms. Jane quit breathing, concentrating on the overpowering desire to just remain as close to Greg as she could.

"Vegetables," she said with the breath that finally escaped her. She tried to pull away. "Vegetables. Pot." She wiggled and pushed her hands against his chest. "Greg." She spoke urgently in a whisper sounding as if she were trying to wake him up.

Greg leaned away. "Right. Hungry children."

"The pot's over there."

She pointed to a cabinet beside the stove. He nodded and moved away. "I'll put the water on to boil, you start unwrapping bouillon cubes."

It tasted good. Whatever it was that Greg threw together in her biggest pot, the Boskells devoured it. He also spread butter on the bread, sprinkled it with garlic, and toasted it in the oven. They had orange juice for a beverage. Jane had that and instant iced tea available.

"Let's have a fire in the fireplace," suggested Caroline.

Jacob did a little dance and turned to Jane with a question on his lips. It lost its vitality before spoken. His feet stopped tapping, his shoulders drooped, and he looked at her with utter sadness written in every line of his round little face.

"I don't suppose you have marshmallows."

Jane shook her head regretfully.

"I don't know how this lady survived before we came along," said Greg. "We're going to have to educate her on how to grocery shop."

"And how to eat," added Tom.

"And cook," added Jake.

"Well, at least I know how to start the fire," she asserted with mock indignation.

She went over to the hearth, picked up the long fireplace matches, struck one, turned a dial in the brickwork with the other hand, and with a whoosh, lit the gas logs.

"Owwwww!" Jacob collapsed on the floor. "She cheated."

Jane sat back on her heels and laughed at Jacob. She started to object to being called a cheater, but suddenly they were plunged into darkness except for the flickering light from the fireplace.

"Power lines down," said Greg.

"Wow!" said Tom. "This is cool."

Amy gave him an exasperated look, but laughed too.

"Good thing you have all those candles," said Caroline.

Jane looked around the room. In the dim shadows she saw the many decorative candles placed to provide color, picked for aesthetic qualities, wicks unlit, dusted once a week. She sighed recognizing the inevitable.

"Okay, but some of the candles are not to be burnt. Let me choose the ones to burn."

"Why? Aren't they all made out of wax?" asked Tom.

"Yes," answered Amy. "But some of them are to look at, not to burn."

"We could look at them burn."

"No," said Amy firmly. "They're too pretty to burn."

One of the boys snorted. Jane didn't know which one.

"It's getting late anyway," said Greg. "Let's light a few candles to see what we're doing and then hop into bed. Is your heat electric, Jane?"

"The furnace is gas but the fans are electric."

"We don't need any fans," said Jake, clearly amazed that anyone would want fans in a snowstorm.

"The fans are part of the heating system," piped up Caroline. "They blow the heat into the rooms."

"I'll take care of the furnace. We don't want it burning away trying to heat what it can't reach. You guys dig out the blankets and make up pallets on the floor."

The boys were tucked into the blankets on the couch, and Greg piled up Jane's stylish floor cushions in a long nest-like structure. Amy and Caroline were to share Jane's big bed with her in the bedroom.

"I'm sorry I don't have more blankets," she apologized to Greg as he made his cocoon on the floor, adding the family's coats to his covers.

"I'm close to the fire," he said. "Don't worry. You have enough blankets on the bed?"

"We'll be all right. We have the electric blanket." Jane grinned at his double take. "Just kidding. I know it won't work."

"They could get the electricity back on before morning."

"In your dreams," she answered as she waved and left down the hall.

nineteen

"Ooo, I like this nightie," said Caroline, swirling around the bedroom in the ankle-length pale purple gown.

"Here, let me roll up the sleeves," offered Amy, who had chosen to wear one of Jane's sweatshirts and matching pants to bed.

Jane came out of the bathroom. The candle she carried added light to the one already sitting on the bedside table.

"Everybody set?" she asked.

Caroline bounced, making it hard for Amy to finish rolling the second sleeve.

"Yes, yes! You have to sleep in the middle."

When they settled in bed, Caroline leaned over to blow out their two candles. She scrambled backward and then burrowed down next to Jane. Caroline moved Jane's arm out of the way and put her curly head on Jane's shoulder. Her little arm wrapped around Jane's middle and gave a squeeze.

"This is fun!" declared Caroline.

"Yeah, it is!" Jane managed to say. She hadn't slept with anyone, ever, that she could remember. Even in the crowded conditions in her family's homes, it was an unspoken rule that she never share a bed with anyone. Another not so subtle rejection from her family.

Amy chuckled. "Has she got you in a death grip yet?"

"Yeah." Jane tightened her arm around the little warm figure beside her. "I kind of like it." A thump resounded from the end of the bed.

"Suggums just joined us," Jane explained. "She doesn't sleep in her bed when it's this cold."

Caroline broke away from Jane's embrace and sat up in bed.

"Here, Suggums, you can sleep with me." She grabbed the

125

dog to pull her up closer. A dog bed partner was no problem to her.

"She probably won't stay, Caro," said Jane. She stopped, wondering over the easy way the nickname had slipped out.

Oh, God, this is so good. I like this.

"Why?" demanded Caroline.

"I don't know," Jane said. She pulled both Caroline and Suggums in closer. The warm, cuddly feeling settled over her again. "Suggums prefers to sleep at the foot of the bed. Did you ever call Betsy about Princess?"

"Uh-huh. While you were in the kitchen with Daddy. Betsy put the phone down to Princess's ear and I talked to her. I told her to be good and I missed her. Betsy said she made a puddle in the kitchen."

"Was Betsy's mom upset?"

"No, but her dad stepped in it. He was upset." Caroline petted Suggums, and the dog curled up on her chest with her chin on Jane's arm. "Tell us a story."

"A story? What about?" asked Jane.

"When you were a little girl. When you were nine like me."

"Hmmm." Now what could she tell this child about the unhappy house she'd lived in? Jane wished Caroline had asked for *The Three Little Pigs.* She vaguely remembered that story.

"Come on," prompted Caroline. "You start with, 'When I was little like you.' It's easy."

"When I was little like you. . . my mother had to stay in bed almost all the time. I would get up in the morning and fix my breakfast all by myself."

"Was she sick?"

"Yes."

"What did she have?"

"A disease called alcoholism," answered Jane truthfully and rushed on to prevent another question. "My father had an early shift. He went to work at three in the morning, so I was by myself."

"Don't you have any brothers and sisters?"

"I have six brothers and sisters but they are all much older than I am, and by the time I was nine, they lived in their own homes with their own families."

"Did they have children?"

"Yes."

"Did—"

"Caro," interrupted Amy. "Quit asking so many questions. Don't you want to hear about the breakfast?"

"I needed background information."

"Well, now you've got it. Be quiet. It's more polite to be a good listener."

"I'm sorry," said Caroline as she patted Jane's stomach.

"It's okay, but Amy's right," said Jane. "I don't have much practice telling stories so you better not interrupt. I get confused and can't remember where I am in the story."

"You were fixing breakfast all by yourself."

"Right. Well, I got out the cereal and the milk, but the milk carton was empty even though it had been in the refrigerator, so I decided to invent a new breakfast. I got out the apple juice and poured that on my cereal."

"Yuck!"

"No, it was pretty good. It was the kind of cereal that makes chocolate milk when you pour regular milk on and so it was very tasty."

"I still say, 'Yuck!' I'm glad Amy and Daddy fix my breakfast. Are we going to have cereal and apple juice tomorrow?"

"No, I don't have any apple juice."

"Caro." Amy's voice warned her little sister to be quiet.

"Anyway," continued Jane, "I got my books and went to school, and I guess that wasn't very exciting because I don't remember much about it. I do remember going to the house down the street on Thursday afternoons. They had a Bible club." Jane rambled through some recollections about her visits at Mrs. Grehurst's and the chores she'd done at home. She paused when she realized how still Caroline had become. Steady, even breathing confirmed her suspicions. Her guest had gone to sleep.

"Is she asleep?" whispered Amy.

"Um-huh," murmured Jane.

"Was that true?"

"About my mother?"

"The whole thing."

"Yes."

"You didn't have much fun, did you?" asked Amy. "Why did you do the dishes and the cleaning and all? Your mother was in bed. She wouldn't care."

"She did get out of bed," said Jane. "While I was at school, she must have gotten out because by the time I came home again she was either gone or drunk."

"That's awful. But why did you do the chores?" Amy persisted.

"Well, my father liked a clean house. He was pretty loud when he found it dirty."

"But didn't he yell at your mother? It was her job."

"It didn't do much good to yell at her, Amy. When she hadn't come home yet from the bar or was too drunk to listen, he yelled at me."

"So you took care of things so your dad wouldn't be unhappy."

"I'm sorry to say, Amy, that I wasn't that interested in my father's state of happiness. I cleaned so I could be happy. I couldn't be comfortable with him yelling and carrying on, so I tried to make things go smoothly in any way I could."

"I sometimes do things so my dad will be happy. I really want him to be happy."

"You love your dad," whispered Jane.

"Didn't you love yours?" Amy whispered back.

Jane paused. It was a hard admission. "No," she said. "I guess I didn't. But I wanted to."

Jane felt a movement under the covers. Amy's hand found her elbow and followed it down to her hand. Amy interlaced her fingers with Jane's and squeezed. Neither one knew exactly what to say next.

"Did your mother die?" Amy asked.

Jane thought of the explanation that Greg had given her the night her aunt had called.

"Part of her died when I was very young. The alcoholism killed the part of her that wanted to take care of me. Eventually, my father stopped living with us, and I didn't know where he was. The people who decide what to do with children who aren't being taken care of properly came and took me away. I lived with each of my older brothers or sisters for awhile, then I went to live with my aunt."

"Was your aunt like your mother?"

"No," she said. "Aunt Nelda ran a bookstore, and lots of philosophers and poets would come and hang around. We lived up an old wooden staircase in the back in an apartment on the third floor. Aunt Nelda always had interesting food, and she'd give me money to go buy clothes sometimes. But she was too busy to take care of me. It was better than at home, but it still wasn't. . .good."

"What would be good?" asked Amy wistfully.

"For someone to smile at me when I came home."

"That's all?"

Jane felt the conversation becoming too heavy for her to handle and sought a way to lighten it.

"Well, that's what Suggums does when I come in. She doesn't smile with her lips, she smiles with her whole body. Her tail wags ninety miles an hour, she wiggles until I pick her up, and if I let her, she licks my face." Amy was quiet and Jane dared to probe a little.

"What would be good for you, Amy?"

"To have someone else be in charge," she said without hesitation.

"Doesn't the oldest sibling often have to be the one in charge?" asked Jane.

"But not like a mother," explained Amy.

"Your father's very proud of your maturity," offered Jane.

"Yeah." Amy let go of Jane's hand and rolled over, her back to the older woman.

Jane felt inadequate. What could she say? She didn't have a clue as to what was wrong, let alone how to comfort the girl. Those words of wisdom she'd prayed for hadn't arrived yet.

Jane reached out a hand and laid it on Amy's shoulder.

"I'm sorry, Amy. I don't understand."

"It's okay," was the muffled reply. "I don't understand either."

❧

"Wake up, sleepyheads!"

Jane groaned and pulled the pillow over her head. *Who in the world let those little banshees in the bedroom?*

"Wake up, wake up, wake up, wake up!"

Suggums started barking. She had the right idea—chase the little shouters out of the room. Jane pulled covers over her head and the pillow.

"We're going to have pancakes and poison syrup!" shrieked one high-pitched voice.

"Good," said Amy grumpily. "You go eat some of the poison syrup now and come back later to tell us what it tastes like."

"It's too cold to get up," complained Caroline.

"Not poison, boysen syrup," said Thomas in his worldly-wise voice.

"Good," uttered Amy again. "Go let Dad put you boys in the syrup. *Then,* you'll be quiet!"

Jane moaned and rolled over. She felt a tug-of-war going on with the blankets on Amy's side of the bed. She figured the boys were using force and she ought to divert the enemy.

"Somebody let Suggums out the patio door," said Jane. The strategy worked.

"Come on, Suggums," called one of the boys. "Come on, wanna go out?" The noise of eight feet trundling down the hall retreated. A moment later the same thundering footsteps advanced.

"There's too much snow. She can't get out."

"Take the shovel from the garage and clear off enough space on the patio for her to go out," instructed Jane from the hollow of her blanket cave. "And hurry. She's been waiting all night."

The footsteps retreated once more.

"I hope Princess is all right," said Caroline.

"You can call," said Amy.

"It's too cold."

"You can pull the phone in under the covers and call," suggested Jane. "But it's on Amy's side. You'll have to crawl over me and her to get to it."

"Okay." The blanket lifted for a moment letting in a draft of frigid air. Jane felt Caroline cross over her midsection and heard Amy's "oomph" as Caroline passed her. In another moment, she heard the dial tone.

"I guess we've got to get up sometime," Jane said to Amy.

"Dad's pancakes really are good."

"If we hurry, we can pull on socks and robes and get to the living room and the fireplace."

"Yeah, it might be warmer in there than it is here."

"Okay," said Jane. "I'll get out first and dig out the socks and a couple of robes. When I've got them ready for you, I'll let you know."

"Okay."

An hour later they were drinking hot tropical punch, having devoured stacks of pancakes with boysenberry syrup improvised from Jane's jam.

"This is good," said Tom, who had expressed great doubts over having this hot drink over cocoa or hot cider.

"What shall we do to pass the time?" asked Caroline. It had been decided earlier that it would be hours before the roads were clear enough for them to make the journey home.

"Let's teach her Whupya," said Jacob.

"Yeah, then we'll whupya good," agreed Tom.

twenty

The busy days melted away faster than the snow. Jane looked at the calendar next to her phone in the kitchen and wondered how the Saturday before Christmas had arrived so quickly. For Jane, Christmas had never been a big holiday. She gave presents to a few of the people at the office. The company sent out Christmas cards to clients. Jane called her aunt on Christmas morning. The activities that went on at church often saved her from total oversight of the season.

This year was different. This year the Boskells were a part of her life. What should she get Greg? Caroline would be easy to pick a present for and the boys would probably be no problem. But what about Amy? What could she get Amy that the young teen would appreciate? And Amy had a birthday too.

The doorbell interrupted her thoughts. She opened the door to find Thomas with tears running down his cheeks and a protective arm around Jacob. Jacob whimpered softly, holding his right arm against his chest and looking dreadfully pale. Tears had dried on his cheeks.

"What happened?" she gasped, at the same time opening the door wider and waving them in.

"We were sledding in the park." Tom gulped back a sob. "Jake hit a tree."

"Go sit in the living room and I'll call your dad," said Jane.

"He's not home," said Tom, a note of panic shaking his voice.

Jane had been headed for the kitchen but she turned at this news just in time to see Jacob sway. She leapt to catch him. Scooping his small frame into her arms, she stood motionless in the hall. What should she do?

"Is your aunt home?" she asked.

"No, nobody's there but Amy."

"Where's Caroline?"

"At Betsy's."

"Call Amy and tell her we're taking Jake to the hospital."

Tom ran to the kitchen phone, and Jane carried Jake in to lay him on the couch.

"Stay down, Suggums," she ordered as she rushed to the back room to change her slippers for shoes. The dog dashed ahead of her. She grabbed her purse and headed back down the hall, Suggums merrily keeping up. The excited fur ball circled the couch twice.

"Amy wasn't there, either," said Tom, standing beside the still form of his brother. Suggums jumped against his leg demanding attention, but he didn't notice her. "I left a message on the machine."

"Good," said Jane and opened the closet door to get her parka. She was pushing her arms into the sleeves when she came back to the couch.

"He's moving," Tom announced.

Jane crouched beside the sofa and put a hand on Jacob's head. She noticed a scrape across his forehead and the beginnings of a bruise underneath the skin. He stirred slightly and moaned. Suggums sat back and looked anxiously from one human to another. She cocked her head and became very still.

"Jake," Jane said soothingly. "Jake, you're going to be okay. We're going to take you to the hospital."

He opened his eyes and squinted at her.

"My head hurts," he complained. "I'm going to be sick."

For a split second Jane wondered how he could know he was coming down with something. Then, his meaning dawned on her, and she reached over to the coffee table and dumped the contents of a ceramic bowl. Pens, paper clips, rubber bands, a nail file, a dog brush, coupons, and an array of other items bounced and scattered over the wooden surface. Jane rolled the injured boy on his side and held the empty bowl under his chin just as he lost the contents of his stomach.

"Eww, gross!" said Tom.

"Tom, go to the bathroom and get a washcloth. Wet it with cold water, wring it out, and bring it back," commanded Jane.

Tom took off with Suggums bobbing along behind him.

"My arm hurts," moaned Jacob. He leaned back again against the throw pillows. His pale skin showed beads of perspiration across his forehead and upper lip.

Jane put the bowl back on the table, shoving the miscellaneous litter out of the way. Gently she ran her hand down his coat sleeve and found a lump halfway down the forearm.

Tom came back with the cloth with Suggums following. Jane wiped Jacob's face.

"I'll be right back," she told the boys. "Hold the bowl for him if he gets sick again," she instructed Tom as she raced down the hall again.

She heard his incredulous "Me?" but didn't stop. Suggums raced at her heels barking excitedly. In her bedroom closet she reached to a top shelf and brought down a box. Pulling it open, she unceremoniously dumped the contents on the bed. Pawing through the summer shorts, skirts, and tops, she grabbed what she was looking for, and again headed down the hall. Suggums followed.

"What's that?" asked Tom.

"It's a tube top. I wear it under blouses. We're going to put it over Jacob's jacket around his midsection to hold his arm still while we move him. I think his arm is broken."

Jacob cried when she sat him up. His skin felt cold and clammy. Tears sprang to Jane's eyes as well, and she had to bite her lip to help her stay calm. She feared she would start bawling, and the boys needed her to be a calm adult. She weighed the option of calling 911, but didn't think it was a life-threatening emergency and knew she'd die a thousand deaths waiting for the ambulance to get there. She'd load him in her car and take him to the emergency room. That would be faster.

Jane carried Jacob to the car in the garage with Tom opening and closing doors and making sure Suggums stayed in the house. She strapped Jacob in the back seat belt and ordered

Tom into the other seat.

"What about a bucket?" asked Tom.

"Bucket?"

"A throw-up bucket. I don't want to be back here with him if he tosses his cookies again."

Jane looked frantically behind her. On the shelf by the door was a small pail she used for gardening utensils. She grabbed it, dumped its contents, and tossed it into Tom's hands. She jerked open the front door of the car, reached across to the automatic garage door opener, and punched the button. She had her seat belt fastened, the car running and in gear before the door was high enough for her to pass under.

Oh Lord, go with us. Help me to drive safely. Don't let anything more happen to Jake.

She reached in her purse and handed the cell phone over the back of the seat to Tom.

"Keep trying to get your dad."

Jane pulled under the awning in front of the hospital emergency entrance minutes later. She switched off the engine and hopped out of the car.

"Stay here." She spoke crisply. She ran through the automatic doors almost before they opened. Four long steps took her to the triage desk. "I need help," she gasped. "I have an injured boy in my car."

The calm nurse turned her head and glanced over a group of people to her left.

"Booker," she barked. When a young black man turned her way, she nodded toward Jane.

He quickly came to her side.

"May I help you, Ma'am?" His deep, soothing voice might have been meant to calm her, but, instead, she felt like shaking him. Couldn't they see she was frantic? Couldn't they tell that handling emergencies was foreign to her? Jane grabbed his arm and started pulling him toward the door.

"Jake hit a tree. I think his arm is broken. He's thrown up. He says his head hurts."

Booker waved a hand at another man. Jane continued to pull Booker out the door and the other man followed with a gurney. Tom opened the back door and hopped out, running to grab hold of Jane's leg. They watched Booker lean into the car and start evaluating Jake.

"Heard you met up with a tree," he said as gentle hands examined the boy. "My name's Booker. What's yours?"

"Jake."

"I'm going to take off this seat belt now. What were you riding?"

"A sled."

"You're going to be all right. Can you tell me where you are?"

"The hospital." He groaned a little as the man lifted his eyelids to check the pupils.

"Yes, you're going to be just fine. What are you wearing over your coat?"

"I dunno."

"This has got you tight enough. Kept you from jiggling. That would've hurt. Looks like you broke your arm. Ever had an X-ray?"

"No."

"Well, that's going to be fun then. My friend is Toby. I'm going to put this collar around your neck before we move you. Then we're going to lift you onto the gurney and take you inside. I'm going to put my arm under your legs like this. You just lie still. Let me do all the work."

In a moment, Booker shifted him onto the gurney and Toby introduced himself.

"You'd better hope I'm better at steering this thing than you were at guiding your sled," Toby teased in an easy manner with a friendly smile on his face. "You're in a great position to see all the pictures Booker, Grace, and I have been tacking on the ceiling. We've got a contest to see who picked the better pictures. All of mine are frogs."

Booker adjusted a strap and nodded to Toby he was ready to go. "Mine are TV space shows. Grace does elephants."

"You just keep your eye on the ceiling as we roll you down the hall. See how many pictures you can spot." Toby turned to Jane. He nodded down the parking corridor. "You can move your vehicle over there. Then check in at the triage desk. They'll bring you back to where we've got Jake."

Tom let go of her and firmly took hold of the side rail of the gurney. "I'm going with my brother," he announced. The defiance in his tone made the two men grin at each other.

"Sure thing," said Booker. "We aren't going anywhere you can't go. I bet you want to see that X-ray machine. Your mom will be along in a minute, and you can keep your brother company."

"Oh. She's not my mom." Tom's voice drifted back to Jane as she opened the car door. "She's my dad's girlfriend."

"Hmm," said Toby. "Your dad's got good taste."

"Nah," said Jake from his prone position. "She can't cook."

Jane's face turned red when Tom identified her as his dad's girlfriend, but the sound of Jake's voice giving his opinion of her cooking brought a sigh of relief. He couldn't be too badly hurt if he still criticized her meals.

Both men laughed as she jumped into the car. Jane pulled the car over to one of the parking places marked Emergency Patients. She jammed the stick shift into park and jerked the keys out of the ignition. Reaching for her purse, she saw how her hand shook and froze. Placing her elbows on the steering wheel and cupping her hands together, she leaned her face into her fingertips and tried to breathe slowly.

Thank You, Father, for getting us here. Please don't let me fall apart. Please help us find Greg and get him here soon.

She took a couple more deep, cleansing breaths and opened her purse. She forced herself to carefully put the car keys into the inside pocket of her bag. She snapped it shut, opened the car door, pushed the automatic lock, and closed the door. She squared her shoulders, willed the trembling feeling from her face, and walked purposefully back to the entrance.

twenty-one

"Can you give Admitting some information?" asked the front desk nurse as soon as she walked through the door.

"I can try," said Jane, pleased her voice no longer quaked. "I don't know about insurance. I'm a friend of the family."

"Hmm," said the nurse and pointed to a hall at the right. "Second desk, Anne. She'll take care of you, then take you down to the boy."

Jane could only give the bare bones information. She didn't even know Jacob's birth date and certainly didn't know his blood type, or if he had any allergies to medicines. She followed Anne down the hall to the room where four curtained beds stood among shiny, intricate machinery. A nurse stood by Jacob's head, taking his temperature with one of those gadgets that probed his outer ear canal.

"Miss Freedman," said Tom just as she came through the door. "I got Dad's foreman at the office, and he's going to drive out to the site to get Daddy and send him here."

"Oh, good job, Tom." Jane felt like the marines were coming to the rescue. The tight feeling of being thrust into responsibility loosened around her heart.

"I just kept dialing and dialing the office until someone answered." He waved her cell phone in the air.

Jane's eyes fell on a pile of bloody clothes. She took a second look at the small form in the bed. Jacob had been stripped of his clothes. A white sheet and blanket lay across his legs. Bandages draped his right arm and an ice pack surrounded them. Her attention quickly transferred to the nurse.

She answered the unspoken question.

"The bone came through the skin."

Jane felt faint. Anne from Admitting guided her to the chair.

"Put your head down between your knees," she instructed

while pushing on the back of Jane's head.

In only a minute, Jane sat up.

"He was bleeding. I didn't even know he was bleeding. He could have bled to death." Her voice was a whisper.

"No," said the nurse who had finished checking her small patient's vital signs. "You did just right to get him here so quickly. If you had dragged that injury out of the arm of his jacket and then moved it again before you loaded him in the car, you would have done a lot of damage. The tube top was inspired." She laughed. "You won't be wearing it again though. We cut it off along with the rest of his clothes."

She'd done the right thing. Jane tried to make sense of it all. If she had bungled through this on her own, she wouldn't be able to say the same thing. When the nurse said "inspired," Jane knew exactly who had guided her actions. She closed her eyes and leaned forward again. The hospital staff may have thought she was faint again, but she was offering up thanks in prayer.

Anne stepped up to the bed and questioned the patient. "Hi, Jake. My name's Anne. Can you tell me your birthday?"

The amount of information Anne drew out of the scared and hurting patient amazed Jane. Tom helped as well. He knew how much his brother weighed and that he had had a tetanus booster the summer before when they both fell through some rotten boards on a deck.

"Remember, Jake," he said through exaggerated clenched teeth. "Daddy said we had to have the shot so we wouldn't have to talk like this for the rest of our lives."

Jacob smiled weakly. He made the face, too. "And so we could still eat pizza and hamburgers and fried chicken."

"Right!"

"Mrs. Boskell," said a voice behind her. A doctor entered the room briskly. He held a clipboard in one hand and reached his other hand out to shake. Jane automatically took the offered hand and was reassured by the firm clasp. His eyes smiled through thick glasses and he seemed relaxed. *To him this must all be routine,* thought Jane, and part of the tension she felt eased with that optimistic notion.

"I'm Dr. Kimbell. We're going to need to X-ray that arm."

"I'm not his mother, just a friend. Someone has gone to locate his father. Can't you get started without him? Can you give him something for the pain?"

"It would help if we knew some medical history. Allergies?"

"Coconut and walnuts," said Tom helpfully.

"Thank you." Dr. Kimbell smiled at him. He turned his full attention to the older brother and hitched up his heavy glasses before speaking again. "Do you know of any medicine your brother is not allowed to take?"

"Aspirin. We're only allowed to take Tylenol."

The doctor nodded his head, accepting the information. In a few moments, Dr. Kimbell took Jane out of the room.

"It's going to take surgery to set that bone. Do you have any idea how soon the father will be here?"

"None."

"Is there some other close relative?"

Jane nodded. "An aunt and grandparents."

"Why don't you try to reach one of them by phone? This isn't a life-threatening situation, but the boy's uncomfortable and we can only do so much prior to surgery. Go back to Anne in Admitting, and she'll help you in any way she can."

"I don't like to leave him." Jane looked through the door. Thomas sat on a round, rolling stool. He occupied himself turning it around and around. The nurse was still with Jake.

"He's fine. We're monitoring him closely, and that big brother of his is a champ!" He took her elbow and turned her down the hall toward the offices. "Go on. Grace won't leave Jake, and I'll tell him you went to call his folks."

Three hours later in a small waiting room on the third floor of the hospital, Jane sat with Greg, Amy, Tom, and the grandparents, Cynthia and Austin Standish. The surgery door solemnly barred them from the information they craved. How was Jacob doing? How much longer would it be? Were there any complications?

Jane prayed to drive off the fruitless questions. With her mind centered on petitioning her Heavenly Father, she warded off unprofitable speculation. A movement caught her attention. She raised her eyes to watch.

Amy stood and moved to the window. She crossed her arms over her chest and stared out over the city. Ponderous clouds sat astride the mountain peaks waiting to dismount into the city. Amy's frown echoed the mood of the sky.

Jane rose and went to stand beside the troubled girl.

"I'm sure he's going to be okay, Amy." Jane lay a hand on the rigid shoulder. "The doctors from the very beginning said it was a bad break, but not something that couldn't mend."

"He might have something wrong with his bones. He might have cancer." Amy reached out a finger and touched the cold pane of the window. Jane felt the girl's spirit was just as cold and fragile as that glass.

"That isn't the most likely outcome of this, Amy."

Amy shrugged, violently wrenching her shoulder out from under Jane's touch. Jane cast a nervous look over her shoulder at the other members of the family gathered in the stark room. Greg held Tom in his lap reading to him from a magazine. Mr. and Mrs. Standish sat together on the couch.

Jane tried again. "Amy, I don't think it's good to think of the worst that could happen. I've been praying to keep my mind running in the right channels—"

"Why are you still here?" The quiet question came out in an explosive hiss. "You aren't family. We don't need you anymore. I don't need you telling me to pray. I know what I'm supposed to do. You can go home now. We can take care of things without you."

Jane saw Greg's head come up and his concerned expression turn their way. She knew he may not have heard what his daughter said, but he must realize there was something awry. She nodded his way, fighting to keep a noncommittal expression on her face. He looked back down at the magazine, and Jane turned her full attention on the rude teenager.

"I don't like being spoken to that way. I was glad to help your brothers. It scared me, but I was grateful that God arranged for me to help. I didn't break into your home and throw myself into your life. I don't know why you've decided I'm your enemy. To me it looks like childish temper. I'm a friend to your family. If you choose to scorn that friendship, then you're the one who's minus a friend. Few of us have enough friends to throw a perfectly good one away."

"That's just it," declared Amy in the same emphatic undertone. "You aren't a perfect friend. You're a lousy substitute. It's Aunt Kate who should be here instead of you. And it's Mom who should be here instead of Aunt Kate."

Amy turned away, purposely glaring out the window and ignoring Jane.

Jane gathered her thoughts and sent up a quick plea for help.

"Amy, the thing you have wrong in this whole situation is this: God hasn't placed me in your life as a substitute for anyone. He has me here in addition to all the others who love you."

"Don't try to tell me you love me."

"No," Jane said sadly. "I don't. Actually, I don't even find you likable. But I keep looking for an Amy I think you're hiding from me. And I think I'd like that Amy."

Amy snorted in response and Jane gave up.

After the surgery, after the good report, Greg took her aside and thanked her.

"Everything seems to be in order now. Cynthia's going to stay with Jacob for awhile. Gramps is going to take Tom. Betsy's mom said she'd keep Caroline and Princess overnight." Greg paused to run a hand through his already disheveled hair. "I'm going to take Amy out for dinner. It's her birthday and we've been too busy to give her much notice." He gave her arm a squeeze and, for a moment, Jane thought he might lean down to brush her lips with a quick kiss. He settled for a warm and grateful smile. "Thanks."

The simple word melted all the turmoil she'd been feeling. Gone was the anxiety of being thrust into this family's trauma; gone was frustration over Amy's behavior. She returned his smile. "You're welcome."

twenty-two

The telephone rang, and Jane rolled under the covers to be closer to the edge of the bed. It rang again before she could make her aching body respond. She reached out one weary arm and plucked the phone from the cradle.

"Heddo," she said.

"Jane?" Greg asked.

"Des," she responded with no enthusiasm.

"You sound horrible."

"Uh-huh."

"Are you going to work?"

"Doh." She sniffed and reached for the tissue box. It was empty. Beside the bed, a small mountain of screwed up white tissue lay in testimony of her horrendous night. Sunday morning she'd felt a scratchy throat when she first opened her eyes. By afternoon, her body told her to hang up her hat; she was in for a first-rate cold.

Greg had called to update her on Jacob's condition and had sympathized in an offhand way. Jane thought he was a bit callous but forgave him since his son had had surgery and his teenage daughter was a general pain. This early morning phone call did nothing to restore him to her good graces.

"Good," said Greg with too much enthusiasm. "You need to rest. Just laze around the house and take it easy."

"Hmm." Jane only grunted.

"Would you mind if I brought Jacob over?"

Jane's eyes popped open and she shook her head slightly to clear it. Mistake. Her full sinuses objected to any movement.

"What?" she managed to croak out.

"Everybody's going every which way today. I can't leave him alone. He's to be still for the next week and the pain

143

medication keeps him pretty low-keyed. I'll bring over a stack of videos, and you can lay on the couch. You at one end and he at the other." Greg tried to paint a cozy picture.

"He'll get my code," objected Jane.

"He was already exposed plenty on Saturday. If he's going to get it from you, it's too late to start precautions now."

Jane didn't want company, especially five-year-old company.

"Greg," she protested. The last of her sentence convulsed in a cough.

"Do you need me to bring you anything, Honey?" he asked in his most sympathetic tone.

Jane knew exactly what she wanted. It was not a kinder-garten companion, but an over-the-counter cold remedy.

"Dat medicine stuff you mix wid hod wader and drink."

"Right," he said briskly. "We'll stop at the pharmacy on the way over." The line went dead.

Jane slowly pushed back the covers and pulled her legs over the side of the bed. Jacob might feel bad enough to lay quietly all day. Was it a sin to hope he did? She felt like death warmed over herself. She headed for the bathroom to take a shower.

ع

Jake lay as lifeless as the afghan that covered him. Jane watched his glazed eyes fixed on the TV screen. They drooped. They closed. Jane hit the stop button on the remote. Jake's eyes remained closed. She depressed the power button and blessed silence filled the room.

The hot liquid medicine had taken the edge off of Jane's discomfort. Jacob hadn't said much after his father settled him on the couch. Her only duty seemed to be to get up and feed the TV a new video periodically. Not too arduous a chore, and before he left, Greg had heated water and brought her a cup of the medicinal brew. He did have a *few* redeeming qualities. She closed her eyes, wanting to sleep the last hour before she could have another dose.

When next she woke, Suggums was still curled up behind

her legs, but Jacob sat cross-legged before the TV with the volume turned way down.

"Hey, Buddy," she croaked.

He looked over his shoulder and grinned.

"You snore," he accused with an impudent smirk.

"Ondee because I've got a code," she explained, a little indignant that she'd been exposed to his mockery. Oh well, at least he'd quietly amused himself while she slept.

"How do you feel?" she asked him.

He shrugged his shoulders, then winced at the pain that shot through his arm. Jane glanced up at the mantel clock.

"Both of us could hab anudder dose of medicine." She forced herself to sit.

"Can I have the graham crackers?" Jacob asked.

Jane nodded.

"And a glass of milk?"

"Did your dad bring milk?"

"Uh-huh," said Jake with the return of that mischievous grin. "He said he wouldn't leave me here without *adequate provisions.*" Jake repeated the last two words with great care, obviously quoting his source of wisdom. He continued with words Jane could almost hear dropping from his father's lips. "You can't trust a gal to have food for an injured boy when you've been in her cupboards and know there's no peanut butter."

Jane smiled in spite of herself.

She got up and dragged one foot after the other to the kitchen. She put the kettle on to boil and poured Jake a glass of milk. She got out a china plate to arrange the graham crackers on and suddenly stopped. She put the glass and a package of crackers on a tray and took it out to her "guest."

"Don't spill dat," she croaked and returned to the kitchen. She made a piece of toast but couldn't swallow it past her raw throat. She ended up with the hot mug of medicine and nothing else. After she gave Jake his pill, she curled up right where she had been before. Maybe she should tell Jacob to back away from the TV. Surely it wasn't good for him to be so close. Well, his eyesight probably wouldn't be ruined in the short time he'd be here, and from that position, he could change the videos without her getting up to do it. Jane stayed awake long enough to sip the last drop from her mug, then laid her head against the cushion and drifted off.

The doorbell rang. Deep within her sleep, Jane complained to God over the invention of bells, doorbells, telephone ringers, alarm clocks, loud trucks. . .

"Should we wake her up?" Caroline's voice penetrated her consciousness.

"No, let her sleep," said Jacob.

Jane gratefully sunk back down into the dreamless void where her eyes didn't burn and itch, her head didn't throb, her throat didn't feel like she'd swallowed sandpaper, and her ears didn't have pressure building behind them. She slept.

&

"Miss Freedman." It was Tom's voice. Funny, she hadn't thought Tom was here.

"Miss Freedman."

"Umm?"

"I broke the catsup bottle."

"Dat's all right, Tom. I don't hab a catsup boddle." Her voice sounded even more raspy than it had earlier. Jane struggled to open her eyes. Tom knelt beside the couch his face inches away from her own. His sincere expression tugged at her heart even in her near comatose state. These kids had penetrated her barriers.

"Dad brought it over with the things for Jake to eat. We were fixing hot dogs," Tom explained.

"It was a *plastic* bottle," added Caroline from somewhere beyond Jane's vision. Her voice held the disdain of an older sister. How could anyone break a plastic bottle?

"A new bottle," added Jake. "It's a big mess."

Jane focused once more on Tom's contrite expression.

"Just clean it up," she mumbled before closing her eyes and successfully closing out their problem as well.

Jane tried to swallow and the effort hurt her ears as well as the swollen tissues of her throat.

I'm going to have to go to the doctor, she admitted.

She heard a crackling and opened her eyes.

"Princess," she croaked.

The puppy lifted her attention from the plastic bag she held between her paws and tilted her head in inquiry.

"What hab you got?" asked Jane, and reached out an arm to take the package from the dog. She couldn't quite reach.

Groaning, she lifted the afghan off her legs and slipped to her knees on the floor. She crawled over to Princess and grabbed the prize just as the puppy realized she'd better run with her loot. It was a half empty hot dog bun bag.

"How many of dese hab you eaten?" she asked the puppy bouncing around her trying to reclaim her treasure. There were five mangled buns left in the wrapper and crumbs on the floor in the pile of her rug. Jane eyed the leftover scraps on the carpet and decided there wasn't a whole bun in evidence.

"You're going to be sick," she told the dog and scooped her into her arms. Jane labored to her feet and put the dog out the back patio door. She then followed the noises she heard coming from her bedroom. Voices and her blow dryer. What could the kids be doing in her bedroom? Why was Suggums barking?

Jane collapsed against the door frame and surveyed the disaster before her.

Perhaps Suggums objected to three Boskell children on her mistress's bed. Or maybe she objected to Tom towel drying her while Caroline simultaneously tried to blow her dry. Or, maybe Suggums didn't like being pink.

"Why is my dog pink?" asked Jane, her voice hoarse.

All motion ceased. Caroline turned off the dryer and avoided her eyes. Jake, sitting with his arm in a sling on a pile of her bed pillows, took that moment to become seriously interested in the view through her window. Tom began to roll the towel in his hands into a tight ball. Suggums grinned, mouth open, tongue hanging out, happy to see her. Jane figured she didn't object to being pink after all.

"She rolled in the catsup," explained Tom in a barely audible voice.

Jane nodded. That would explain it. She remembered something about a broken catsup bottle.

"The catsup?" Jane prodded with her question.

"In the kitchen," explained Caroline. "I went to pick her up because she was licking it off the floor, and she rolled over for me to rub her belly."

Yes, Suggums would have turned belly-up in her submissive posture if she thought she was in trouble. Jane walked over to peer into her bathroom.

"Does the kitchen look as bad as the bathroom?" she croaked.

"Worse," mumbled Tom.

"Clean," ordered Jane. Her voice held little emotion, and the children quickly passed a look of doubt between them. Was she angry?

Caroline slipped off the bed first and sidled into the bathroom past the sick grown-up. Tom followed. Jane went over to the bed and sat on the edge.

"You okay?" asked Jacob.

She nodded.

"We're sorry."

"It's okay."

She leaned back and pulled her legs up so that she laid in the fetal position next to Jacob. He pulled a pillow out from under him and generously offered it to her. It was almost too much effort to lift her head and tuck it under, but Jane managed.

"You want me to get you something?" asked her fellow sufferer.

"Nah."

Jacob scooted his bottom down, careful not to jar his arm, and relaxed against the pillows.

"Daddy should come soon."

Jane tried to think of an answer but her mind fogged on her and only wisps of thought traveled through.

"Would you like a hot dog?" he asked.

"Nah."

"That's what we were doing when the catsup bottle fell off the top shelf of the refrigerator. Tom opened the door and it just jumped out and hit the floor with a *kebam!* You should have seen it. It was plastic, too." Jacob stopped, obviously puzzling over the vagaries of life. A plastic catsup bottle had betrayed them. "Boy, did it splatter." He resumed the gory account. "There was the puddle on the floor and splashes on the cabinet, and drips on the wall clear across the room. Then we were standing there and it started dripping catsup. It was on the ceiling, only it was coming off in drips."

Jane heard the mixture of amazement and glee in his voice and closed her eyes tighter. Her person was not cut from mother material.

"Caroline," she whispered.

"Caroline!" Jacob echoed. His voice tore through her eardrums. "Miss Freedman wants you."

Caroline dropped the rag she'd been using to mop the floor in the tub and flew to her side.

"Sweedie, could you make a packet of dat code medicine?"

"Sure," said Caroline.

"Be real careful. I don't want you to burn yourself."

"Okay."

A few minutes later, Jane sat in the stuffed rocker by her bedroom window, wrapped in an afghan and sipping medicinal brew from an elegant mug. Suggums curled up in a ball half on her leg and half on the cushiony arm of the chair. Jane tried to ignore the sounds coming from the kitchen and gazed at the sleeping figure on her bed. Jacob looked sweet, angelic even, asleep on her flowered bedspread. Jane tried not to imagine what the other two "angels" were doing in her kitchen.

"Caroline said the vacuum cleaner word," announced Tom in an indignant whisper.

Jane's eyebrows shot up. "The vacuum cleaner word?"

"Yeah." Tom nodded his head hard enough to ruffle his hair. "We're not allowed to say the vacuum cleaner word, the cigarette word, the barnyard word, and a whole bunch of others. She said the vacuum cleaner word."

By that time, Jane had a fairly good idea she didn't want clarification as to just exactly what these words were. Her eyes went automatically to the clock by her bed. Would this day ever end? Would that man ever come back to claim his children and get them out of her house?

"Well, send her in here to me and I'll talk to her about it."

Now what am I going to do?

A pouting Caroline came back with eyes narrowed and lips pursed to express her displeasure.

"Why are you saying things you shouldn't?" asked Jane.

"I keep scrubbing the red stains and they don't come off and Tom's no help. He just gave up. Now the paint is coming off."

Jane sighed. Looking closely at Caroline, she thought of a number of things to say, but none of them were nice and all of them were too much trouble to say with her throat feeling like it did. A tear formed at the corner of Caroline's eye and all of Jane's resentment crumbled.

"It's okay, Honey. You tried your best."

Caroline plopped into Jane's lap, pushed Suggums out of the way and cried against Jane's shoulder.

"I'm sorry. I'm so sorry. I was going to make you and the boys hot dogs for dinner and everything went wrong."

Jane patted her shoulder.

"It's okay. It's okay."

All Jane wanted was to go to sleep, alone in her house with only her dog for company.

"You go take Suggums out for me, Caroline. I'm going to curl up with Jacob and sleep until your daddy gets here."

Greg Boskell did finally come get his children. All Jane remembered of his visit was a kiss on her forehead and a promise to paint her kitchen.

twenty-three

"You don't even have a Christmas tree?" Bunny put the cumbersome, brightly wrapped package she carried down on Jane's coffee table and began to peel off her gloves, scarf, and heavy coat. "Is this a 'this year thing' because you've been ill, or are you this pathetic every year?"

Jane tossed her an aggravated look and took the coat.

"It's not pathetic," she objected. "It's just practical. Why put up a tree for one person?"

Bunny shook her head in despair.

"There's no dealing with you sometimes. I know your upbringing was irregular, but you have a tendency to overdo the 'raised without family and tradition' bit."

"Did you come over here on Christmas day to harass me about my lifestyle?" Jane threw the coat over a chair upholstered with dainty flowers on a cream background and sank into the matching one. She snapped her fingers at Suggums, distracting the dog from her examination of the package, then patted her lap to invite Suggums up. If her guest was in a belligerent mood, it would feel good to hide behind the little scrap of fur.

"Well, sit down," Jane urged her friend and coworker.

"You must be sick, Girl," said Bunny, dropping her plump frame into the cushions of the couch.

"Why?"

"You just put my coat on a chair instead of hanging it up."

Jane sighed and grimaced good-naturedly. Bunny always poked at what she called her "characteristic persnicketiness" in hopes of loosening the tight hold Jane kept on her life. Jane shook a mock fist at her guest, ending the gesture by scooping Suggums up from her lap and holding her firmly against her chest.

151

"I've had strep throat," Jane said by way of explanation. "A *bad* case of strep throat."

"Yes," said Bunny, who knew full well why Jane hadn't been at the gallery all week. "I've got some chicken soup to bring in from the car. Don't laugh. It'll do you good. It's been medically proven now. All those mothers pushing their chicken soup were right on target."

"I'm getting better." Her defensive tone pushed at Bunny to keep her distance, but Bunny chose not to take the hint. Their relationship in business was concrete. In life outside the office, Bunny had had to press for every toehold in the younger woman's world. After years of determination, Bunny was the closest thing to a real friend Jane had.

"You'll be even better when you've had the soup. Now open your present."

Jane put the dog down and proceeded to carefully pull the red embossed foil wrapping off of the large heavy box.

"Rip the paper," urged Bunny.

"No," Jane answered. She proceeded with her usual respect for the beautiful package. At last the paper fell away.

"A bread machine?" Jane looked up at her friend. "You always give me a book."

"I did this year, too. There's a recipe book inside. Read the box."

"What do I want with a bread machine?" asked Jane, unable to hide her surprise. "I mean, I don't cook, Bunny. You know that."

"It's about time you started. This is relatively painless. All you have to do is measure in the ingredients and push the buttons. The results are great with a minimum of effort."

"Well, thanks," said Jane, trying to sound like she meant it.

Bunny smiled with a smugness Jane couldn't quite trust.

"So where are the handsome widower and his tribe today?" Bunny asked.

"Taking my old couple out to dinner for one thing."

Bunny quirked an eyebrow.

"You know I always take an old couple from church out on holidays. Today it was to be the Jenkinses, and I'm not fit to go out so the Boskells are pinch-hitting for me."

"And they're coming over later?"

Jane shook her head in the negative as she pried the huge staples out of the top of the box and lifted the cardboard flaps.

"So, they were here earlier?"

"No." Jane lifted the top piece of cardboard out of the box and pulled out the cookbook.

"Jane, look at me," ordered Bunny.

Jane lifted her eyes.

"What happened to the slight thawing of your heart I detected a week ago?"

"I caught cold."

"Your heart has frozen over again because of a virus?" Bunny hurled her shoulders back against the cushions, gestured dramatically with her arms, and rolled her eyes. "Give me a break!"

"I am not mother material, Bunny. It won't work out. I don't like the idea of being called upon to wipe runny noses, fix three square meals, watch soccer games, and put my own comforts aside in order to baby-sit exuberant small people. I've been given the opportunity to try it out and I failed miserably."

"You did pretty well as an EMT for the broken arm."

"I was petrified."

"No, petrified means you don't move. You made all the right moves."

"By accident," she protested.

"Through God's guidance." Bunny clamped her jaws together on any further diatribe she might want to deliver.

Jane opened the recipe book and thumbed through the pages. She deliberately ignored the woman stewing on her couch. She had no intention of pursuing this conversation or allowing any encouragement of Bunny's pursuit. Her strategy failed.

"You love that man," Bunny added through clenched teeth.

Jane groaned and closed the book with a snap.

"I could love that man," she explained with exaggerated patience. "I don't have to."

Bunny's expressive eyebrows shot up her forehead. "This I find very interesting. You have this unique ability to turn love off and on like it was coming out of a faucet? You can even turn the handle and adjust the flow so only a trickle of love pours forth?"

"Look, Bunny, I've known you what, four years?"

"Five."

"Five years. Have you ever known me to become involved in anyone's life?"

"Church."

"Church is safe. I can waltz into someone's life and step out graciously without making any bonds. Take some old people to lunch three or four times a year and only then. Smile politely and shake hands in Sunday school. No ties, no commitments. Are you beginning to get the picture?"

Bunny stared at her friend, clearly realizing that what she outlined so starkly was true. Jane did have her routine down pat. The routine excluded close ties.

"You can't be happy that way," Bunny objected.

"I can, and I am," Jane declared. "I'm just not you, Bunny, even though I admire your warm connection with people. I am, at heart, an isolationist. I was raised in an emotional vacuum. It is *hard* for me to relate."

"It doesn't sound very comfortable, Jane."

"On the contrary, it is extremely comfortable."

"Maybe comfortable wasn't the right word," admitted Bunny. "It sounds lonely, sterile, unsatisfying."

"It's always been comfortable for me, Bunny. I had God as my Father, my Friend, my Comforter, and my Teacher. He was my everything."

"Why are you using the past tense?" asked Bunny, a frown of concern furrowing her brow.

"Because with the entrance of Greg Boskell and his motley

crew, I've lost my focus."

"You think you're less of a Christian?"

"Yes," Jane exploded. "I feel less connected, more vulnerable, less sure, more fragile. This can't be good, Bunny. It just can't!"

Bunny sat thinking. She didn't have immediate answers for her friend, yet her expression showed her suspicion about what may be wrong.

"What if this is all God's plan? What if God thinks it would be better for you to be less comfortable and more involved?"

Jane snorted in a very unladylike manner. "How could it be God's plan to move me away from Him?"

"Well, this is Christmas," said Bunny. "Seems like a good time to ask some Christmas-type questions. Why did God send Jesus to earth?"

"To reveal His love and His plan for salvation," Jane shot back.

"Good answer. But, being God, couldn't He have arranged some other means without coming among us and actually physically touching humanity?"

"I guess. Nothing is impossible for God."

"Yet He chose to move among the people."

"Yes," agreed Jane cautiously.

"And you think God is satisfied with your Christianity in an isolated form where you aren't required to rub shoulders with us mortals."

"I didn't say that!"

"I don't think God is pushing you out of the nest to get rid of you, but to give you the opportunity to grow."

"Now I'm a bird in a nest." Jane's face reflected the control she tried to keep on her emotions. Bunny's reasoning shook her tight security. She'd rather scoff at the advice than succumb to it.

"I think you've been the bird trying to stay in the egg." Bunny shook her head sadly from side to side. "It won't work. It isn't natural to not grow."

"I had a big dose of reality earlier this week, Bunny." Jane's voice pleaded her case. "Three of the Boskell children were left in my care. Well, actually just one, the other two and a dog just came along later, supposedly to help out. Their own idea.

"I told you all about it. It was a fiasco. It was the three nicer children. Antagonistic Amy wasn't even among them. I not only didn't take care of them, I allowed them to create havoc. And I resented it, Bunny. I didn't like having them here. I didn't enjoy playing mother. I raged inwardly at Greg for imposing on me."

"So because you had a few negative feelings you think you failed?"

"Yes." Jane reopened the recipe book as if she were suddenly interested in reading the book from cover to cover.

Bunny persisted.

"That would be valid if it were true that mothers feel motherly twenty-four hours of every day. Moms resent children from time to time. Good moms get tired of the duties and responsibilities. It's called being human. It does not cross you off the list of motherhood candidates just because you were grumpy while you were sick."

"There are too many areas I fall short," complained Jane.

"So you were the best interior designer the day you graduated from college?" Bunny asked sarcastically. "You can learn."

"It's not learning, Bunny. It's changing! I'd have to *be* another person."

"So? God's in the business of changing people. Haven't you heard?"

Jane sat quietly. Suggums jumped into her lap and insisted on being stroked. She curled up in a comfortable position and leaned until she had successfully turned over exposing her underside for the pleasure of a good rub. Jane caressed the fur with a firm light movement. It steadied her nerves.

"What if I go to all the trouble and it's not enough?" she asked in a soft, fearful voice.

"Honey, who's going to be the judge of whether or not it's enough? You, Greg, the kids, that Amy, God? Who's the one that really matters?" She went on, answering her own question. "You aren't going to disappoint God, Jane. He's already counted you as worthy."

"I really don't want to do this, Bunny."

"I know you're afraid, but I think you *do* want to do it. If you get past the fear, you'd even enjoy the challenge." Bunny smiled, her eyes sparkling with the dare she presented to her friend. "Just think how you like rearranging things—walls, drapes, colors, windows. . . . This would be designing a life, not just a room."

"And what if I mess it up?"

"First, you have the Master Designer as a partner. Put a little faith in Him. Second, you're good at what you do. Have a little confidence in yourself. Third, if you mess up, tear the project down and begin again."

"Somehow I think this is an oversimplification of the situation."

"Somehow I think you'd be better off tackling the mole hill instead of cowering before mountains."

Jane grinned in spite of herself. "Your analogies leave a lot to be desired."

Bunny shrugged.

"Okay. What do you suggest I do first?" asked Jane.

Bunny grinned, her smile splitting her face and showing two rows of beautiful white teeth.

"Bake a loaf of bread."

twenty-four

"I'm bringing over garlic bread, meatballs, and spaghetti sauce, but you have to boil the pasta," Jane told Greg over the phone. "I made it myself under the tutelage of Bunny. But I don't know how to cook the noodles, so you have to do that."

Greg's warm laugh coming through the line made the smile on Jane's face widen.

"You're on, Honey. How long before you can get it all together and be here?"

"Ten minutes," Jane promised and hung up.

❧

"Bunny has taught me to make meat loaf," Jane crowed into the phone.

"Meat loaf, that sounds exciting," Greg's tone of voice implied a less than enthusiastic response.

"It is," insisted Jane. "I wasn't going to tell you because it is rather a silly name, but it's called 'Fluffy Meat Loaf under a Cloud.' "

"Fluffy Meat Loaf under a Cloud," he repeated, the skepticism in his voice doubled.

"With a gold lining," she continued on a less exuberant note. "Gold, not silver."

"Definitely gold. It's good," she defended her main dish.

She'd been cooking with Bunny for almost a month and had developed a healthy interest in the culinary arts. So far, she hadn't burnt anything. "It's a recipe from the fifties. The bottom layer is meat loaf and the top is mashed potatoes."

"And the gold?"

"Cheddar cheese."

Her eagerness brought a laugh from the other end of the line.

"Greg Boskell, do you want to bring the family to eat, or

not?" she asked indignantly.

"We're coming to your house this time?"

"If I don't rescind the invitation."

"I'll be good," he promised and then explained, "my experience with meat loaf is it turns out like a brick."

An idiotic grin spread over her face. Just maybe she had finally fixed something better than Greg could himself. Bless Bunny and a month of cooking lessons.

❧

Her cinnamon sticky buns passed muster.

The apple pie and beef stew drew rave reviews from her culinary testers.

The family giggled when she announced she was serving Tex-Mex tators but gobbled them down in record time.

Chicken and dumplings earned hugs and kisses.

The pigs in blankets were only slightly more brown than necessary and that was because Greg distracted her with a most devastating series of kisses.

The brownies made up for the crumbly oatmeal cookies made the week before.

❧

"This is the big test, Greg," she announced as she opened the door.

"What's the surprise you cooked tonight?" he asked. Caroline and the boys pushed past her as he collected his greeting kiss.

"Daddy!" Caroline squealed from the kitchen.

"Pizza!" shouted the boys in unison.

Greg grinned at her. "You're ready to be a mother." He gave her an extra kiss of approval.

❧

Valentine's Day. Even though the cold rain poured out of the dark night sky, Jane turned up the radio in her car and sang the love song. A few more blocks and she'd be home. She'd had a great day and it was going to get better. Greg was coming over at nine for dinner. This time when she lit the candles and turned down the lights, it wouldn't be to hide what she was serving. Tonight was destined to be perfect.

She turned the corner next to the park and her headlights picked up a figure darting across the road. Who'd be running pell-mell into the park at this time of night and in this freezing rain? Jane slowed the car and peered into the darkness. Street lamps gave out just enough light for her to watch the sodden person slip, struggle to her feet, and race on to the rocket structure. Jane came to a full stop by the side of the road.

The slight female figure looked disturbingly like Amy Boskell. Jane peered through the darkness in all directions. No one chased her, yet the flight across the street into the park had seemed frantic. Jane turned off the motor and pushed in the button to extinguish her headlamps. She watched the rocket edifice. No movement.

Even if the girl was not Amy, there was something wrong here. Jane zipped up her parka and put the hood over her hair.

In one minute, she was at the base of the playground equipment and soaked from her feet to where her parka ended at the thigh. Peering up through the spiraling metal steps filling the interior of the metal structure, she thought she saw movement at the top.

"Amy?" she called. No answer. "I'm coming up."

The rocket's cold metal sides sloped outward to make a bulge in the middle and then tapered to a point at the top. A platform in that cone allowed children to look out the small round windows. From the base to that pinnacle, there was no space where a little child could slip through and fall to the ground. Nice for a child but claustrophobic for an adult. Jane wished she were Alice and could take a bite of the "Eat Me" biscuit.

It didn't make much sense to keep calling "Amy" to someone who might not be Amy, so Jane concentrated on working her way up the steps.

Quarter-sized holes riddled the sides. Cold wind and rain blew through these openings. Inside her knitted gloves her fingers grew numb. The wind and rain battered the metal frame. Thin sheets of metal creaked as they pulsated under the bombardment. The darkness enveloped her so completely she held on to the rail circling the interior wall of the rocket and felt for each step with her foot.

Oh, Father in heaven, this is scary. Please direct my steps. And when I get to the top, let it only be one scared girl waiting there.

As she neared the last few feet, Jane heard sobs.

"Amy?"

"Go away!"

Jane crouched in the small space.

"Amy, I can't see you. Where are you?"

"Go away."

Jane reached toward the voice and found her huddled in a ball.

"Oh, Amy, what's wrong?" She instinctively gathered the shivering child into her arms and was surprised when Amy shifted against her. The little girl's arms went around her and embraced her in a death grip. The sobs intensified and the poor child shuddered with each breath.

Jane sat beside her and held her firmly.

"There now. Don't cry so. It's going to be all right. You're not alone. Whatever it is, you're not alone."

Jane continued to hold and rock the crying girl until the great sobs became quieter. Amy still shivered violently.

"We have to get out of here, Amy," she said. "You're cold. Let's go down and to my car. You'll be warmer. I'll take you home. Come on now."

She coaxed Amy down the steps, through the pelting rain, and over to her car.

"I don't want to go home! I can't go home!" Amy protested wildly.

"Then we'll go to my place," Jane assured her. "You don't have to go home until you're ready."

Dear Father, what is this all about? Is she pregnant? Is it drugs? I don't think so. What should I do for her? Should I call Greg? Should I call the youth pastor at church?

Jane heard no voice in the torrent of rain. But she did know what to do. Get the freezing child warm and calmed down. Yes, she'd call Greg, but God had put Amy in her path and Jane would offer her comfort. If Greg wanted to call someone else, that was his decision.

She drove in silence to her driveway and hit the button of the automatic garage door opener. Amy continued to cry, quieter now but with an intensity that frightened Jane.

Without trying to get the girl to talk, Jane persuaded Amy to come in the house. She talked her out of the wet clothes and into a warm tub of water. Finally Amy quit shivering, but still the tears streamed down her cheeks. In the bathroom, Jane left the same sweatshirt and pants that Amy had worn the time she had slept at her house. Leaving her soaking, Jane went to call Greg.

"The water's cold now, Amy," Jane spoke softly. The crying had stopped, but Amy lay listlessly in the water. Jane picked up a big towel. "Come on, out of the water. I've turned on the electric blanket. I'll tuck you in."

She didn't move. Jane pushed the lever next to the faucet opening the drain.

"Please, Amy, I want to help you."

Slowly, the girl stood. Jane wrapped the towel around her skinny body thinking she looked too pale and delicate. She supported her as she stepped over the edge of the tub and ended up rubbing the towel vigorously over her fragile frame. It took patience and persistent urging to get Amy into the clothes and across the room to the bed. When she was tucked in, Jane sat on the bed beside her and took her cold hand to hold.

"I called your father. He's out searching for you, but he'll be here as soon as he gets my message."

Amy's eyes fixed on her face.

"Can you tell me what happened?" asked Jane.

"Aunt Kate is getting married," Amy whispered.

"To Dave?"

Amy nodded. "They came over to the house. It's Valentine's Day and he asked her this morning. He came to Grandma's house at dawn with a basket of roses and the ring. He sang to her from the garden in the back of the house. She's *happy*."

Amy's voice broke on the last word. She pulled her hand out of Jane's and turned away, rolling her small body into a tight ball. Jane stroked her back.

"Why did you want her to marry your dad?" she asked.

"Because then it would be like it was before my mom died."

"Your aunt isn't like your mom. Your grandmother told me that. Your father told me that. And even Kate told me the same thing."

"It doesn't matter. She'd be there at night, not just during the day. She'd have more time for us. We'd be important to her. She'd love us. She'd love us like our mother." Amy began to cry softly again and turned her head into the pillow. "Mommy."

Jane heard the last word uttered with a feeble moan, and tears sprang to her eyes. She reached out a hand and gently stroked the damp hair away from Amy's face. Jane prayed. It was some time before she had the confidence to speak.

"When Jake had his accident and we were waiting for his surgery to be over, you told me not to tell you I loved you. Do you remember that?"

A small nod showed Amy had heard her and remembered.

"And I told you that I didn't love you and I didn't even find you likable."

No response, but the crying had stopped. Jane continued to gently smooth Amy's red hair.

"That was not quite two months ago. Things have changed."

Jane felt Amy tense as if she were waiting for the next words to hurt her.

God, help me say the right things. I know she doesn't need to be admired for her maturity. She needs to be loved for being a little girl. She needs to be back in that place where a mother loved her.

"I've seen you two or three times a week when I tried out the results of my cooking lessons on your family. I've seen you laugh and help your brothers and sisters. I've seen you play with the dogs. You're kind and gentle. I think you're the most wonderful little girl I've ever known."

"I'm not a little girl," she whispered.

"Not all the time," agreed Jane. "But all of us are little children some of the time. I sometimes feel afraid, lost, alone."

Amy shifted slightly so that she could look at Jane.

"When I'm with your family," Jane continued, "I don't feel that way anymore. You're important to me. I love your daddy, Amy. I love Caroline, Thomas, and Jacob. I love you."

"I haven't been nice to you."

"I don't love you because of the things you do. I just love you."

"You can't."

"Yes, I can." Jane spoke firmly her eyes focused directly on Amy's sad green eyes. Amy flinched, her teeth worried her lower lip, and a small gasp escaped.

Amy sprang up and her arms encircled Jane's neck. The sudden movement knocked Jane back, but she recovered and enclosed the slight child in a loving embrace.

"I want my mommy so bad," Amy sobbed.

Jane gave a deep sigh of relief. Amy cried again but these were gentle, healing tears. Jane cuddled her.

"I know," she whispered against Amy's ear. "I spent years wanting my mommy too."

After awhile, Amy's tears ceased. She breathed evenly, but her eyes didn't close. She rested against Jane's shoulder.

"You know something, Amy," Jane whispered.

"Hmmm?"

"I just realized that as much as I wanted my mom back then, I want your family now. I feel my heart tear a little if I think of moving away or not being able to see you." She squeezed Amy in a warm hug. "Will you share what you have with me?"

Silence followed the question. Jane held her breath.

"Yes," was the whispered reply.

&

"Jane, Amy?" Greg's voice rang down the hall.

"Back here, Greg." Jane stood up and Greg barreled into the room past her and knelt beside the bed where he had gathered Amy into his arms. "I was scared half out of my mind, Amy," he said.

Jane left the room and quietly closed the door behind her.

Greg found her in the kitchen.

"Thank you," he said. "May I use the phone?"

She nodded and continued to tear the lettuce into little pieces and place them in three bowls.

"I need to call home and tell them she's all right."

She nodded again. He made the call quickly and then picked up a knife to help slice the cucumbers into the bowls.

"You may have saved her life tonight."

"Oh, Greg, I don't think it was that desperate."

"I do," he insisted. "I'm not talking about physical danger. She could have caught pneumonia or been taken by some low-life perverts, but I really wasn't thinking about her being physically hurt tonight. I'm talking about saving her life, her future life." Greg put the knife down and ran his fingers through his hair. "I guess I'm not explaining this very well. But she talked to me in there, Jane, really talked to me like a kid to her dad. She didn't sound like an adult conversing to another adult she just barely knows. She was my baby. I knew there was something not right, but I never could put my finger on it."

"Now you know?"

"Yes." A sigh came from him so deep that he shuddered as he released it. "She was trying to be Kathy, to take her place, and she desperately wanted Kate to step in and take the responsibility off her shoulders. That's not what she said but it's what she meant. Everybody praised her for her actions when Kathy died, and she thought she had to keep it up. In one fell swoop she lost her mother and her childhood."

"What are you going to do now?"

"Well." Greg let out a more controlled breath of air. "I'm going to keep her talking and relieve her of some of the responsibility that I've allowed her to take on just by being unobservant. I'm going to make sure she knows it's not her responsibility to keep me happy, keep the family running smoothly, and raise her siblings."

"Would you be wanting some help with that?" asked Jane as she carefully cut thin slices of celery on the cutting board.

"A professional counselor?"

"Do you think she needs that kind of help?"

"Maybe."

"Well, let's get some hot food into her. I have salad, Irish beef stew, and homemade bread."

Greg put his arm across her shoulders and kissed her forehead.

"I was going to propose to you tonight," he whispered.

"You're not going to now." She couldn't keep the disappointment out of her voice.

"No, I'm going to wait a bit. You deserve a proposal that'll knock your socks off. Not one delivered in the midst of a crisis."

"Are you going to bring me flowers at dawn and serenade me from the garden?"

Greg groaned and dropped his forehead to rest against hers.

"Amy managed to tell you that, huh?"

"Uh-huh." She smiled, the twinkle returning to her eyes.

"We'll see." He kissed her briefly and went back to urge Amy out of bed.

twenty-five

"So it's Amy who has come between us again," Jane vigorously chopped the onion in Bunny's kitchen.

"Hey," objected Bunny, "be careful. You're going to have the tip of one of your fingers in the quiche."

Jane scraped tiny bits of onion into the measuring cup.

"I thought you and Amy had come to some kind of understanding on Valentine's Day."

"Yes," admitted Jane as she rinsed the fresh spinach in the sink. "She's more tolerant of my presence, but Greg's so involved in helping her back on the right track that he neglects me." She slammed the loose leaves into the colander. "And doesn't that sound selfish and immature?"

"Actually, it does." Bunny came over and rested a forgiving arm around Jane's shoulders. "Waiting is the hardest thing God ever asks us to do. Don't get down on yourself just because you're human."

"I guess when Amy said she would share her family with me, and then we had that cozy dinner together, I expected that everything would be okay from then on."

"Naïve."

"Thanks."

Bunny laughed.

"Are you up to making pie crust from scratch or do you want to cheat? I have frozen in the deep freeze."

"I want to cheat." Discouragement infiltrated and sabotaged her desire to be a wonderful cook.

"Okay. I'll be back in a minute."

Bunny opened the door to the cellar and descended the steps. When she came back, she tossed a package on the counter in front of Jane.

"It's broken," said Jane.

"Uh-huh. We can fix it though." Bunny turned on the stove. "It's not as good as crust made from scratch and tossing it on the counter like that was almost a guaranteed disaster."

Jane wiped her hands on a kitchen towel and turned to face Bunny, giving Bunny her full attention.

"So why did you toss it?"

"To illustrate a point." Bunny's eyes riveted to Jane's. "You can take the time to work at a crust. You put good ingredients in it. You don't freeze it. You have a great crust that won't fall apart on you. One that will give you pleasure."

"And this relates to. . . ?"

Bunny let out an impatient whoosh of air. "Your relationship in the Boskell family. You can take shortcuts and end up with an inferior product. Or, you can be patient, put in the right ingredients, work the dough, and don't take the easy way."

"Did you use this in some Sunday school object lesson?"

Bunny grinned. "Yep."

"Well, it's pretty good. I'll try to be more patient."

Jane looked at the broken pie crust.

"So, do I have to make pie crust from scratch now?"

"Your decision," answered Bunny.

❧

"Dogs are happier if they know what they're expected to do," the instructor announced.

"That's what Daddy said," Caroline tugged on Jane's arm to be sure she heard.

Suggums sat sedately at Jane's feet, but Princess bounced and tried to reach another dog in the circle that made up the Dog Obedience Class. Suggums had never been to a formal class, and Jane thought sure they would pick up some good tips.

Princess kept escaping the fenced backyard, and Greg was afraid she'd get run over. Coming when called was not her idea of a good game. "Chase down the street" was.

Each dog and owner walked in turn down the center of the

room. Caroline was almost in tears when she finally tugged Princess over the finish line.

"It's okay, Caro," Jane who had gone earlier with Suggums told her. "That's why we're here. Princess is a smart dog and she'll pick it up quickly. We'll practice in the park." Caroline tucked her hand in Jane's and stood quietly beside her with her head down. Within thirty minutes, the talented instructor had Princess trotting beside her owner, and Caroline's chin up with a broad, proud grin on her face.

"Wait 'til we show Daddy, Princess," Caroline exclaimed in the car on the way home. "Thank you for taking me, Miss Freedman."

"You're welcome," said Jane.

I'm applying for the job of their mother, and these kids still call me Miss Freedman.

"Maybe we could think of something else for you to call me, Caro. We've been friends now for a long time."

"No," answered Caroline emphatically. "I already asked Daddy and he said we weren't to call grown-ups by their first names. It shows disrespect."

"Oh," said Jane disappointed. "Well, we'll do what your dad thinks best."

"Don't worry about it, Miss Freedman. Daddy's working on something to fix it."

"Something to fix it?" She cast Caroline an inquisitive look.

"It's a secret. It has to do with Aunt Kate's wedding to Uncle Dave."

"Dave can be called Uncle Dave, but I have to remain Miss Freedman."

Caroline's smile stretched making the dimples in her checks stand out. "Yep!" She sobered. "Don't trick me into telling. I promised. It was Amy's idea and the boys are in on it too."

"Amy's idea?" Jane lost confidence in the speculation she'd made only minutes before. For an exciting moment, she'd thought she'd get to be Mommy instead of Miss Freedman. But if Amy thought it up, what could this mysterious project be?

Jane frowned. Greg hadn't said a word about marriage since Valentine's Day, and two months had already slipped by. In that time period, though, Jane had become more involved with the family. She cooked for them regularly; she attended the school performance night for Jake and Tom. She was greeted with hugs and kisses by everyone except Amy.

Jane smiled. Last Thursday night she had helped Amy hem a skirt she was making for Home Economics class, and Amy had given her a shy hug with a thank-you.

"Patience," she muttered under her breath. "Patience."

❧

The excitement generated by the four Boskell children hit Jane the minute Greg opened the van door and assisted her into the front seat. All four began talking at once. Amy gave up, rolling her eyes and settling back in her seat behind the driver.

"Have they been bouncing like this all morning?" Jane asked Greg when he opened the door and climbed in.

He grinned. "It's an exciting day."

"They look so nice to be so wound up."

"Everybody but me is wearing new duds," explained Greg. "Can't go to your aunt's wedding in last year's styles."

"These are going to double as our Easter clothes, Miss Freedman," Caroline offered as further explanation.

"Everybody looks very nice." Jane smiled at each one.

"Put on your seat belt, Woman," commanded Greg. "We've got places to go and people to see."

The children sat with great decorum in the church pew. Jane sensed that they were more excited about the reception to follow than the lovely church ceremony. Somehow, when they sat down, the children managed to separate Greg and Jane. Jane and Amy sat next to the aisle with Caroline and the boys between them and Greg. Jane looked past the row of heads to where Greg sat watching the vows being exchanged. He turned and caught her looking at him and winked. She blushed, and turned her attention back to what the preacher said.

Weddings are supposed to make you happy, right? I feel so

*depressed. The kids are interested in everything that's hap-
pening. Greg seems content, and I'm a party pooper. What's
wrong with me? I've never felt resentful at weddings in the
past. I guess I want to be the one getting married.*

*Will Greg ever remember he was going to ask me to marry
him? Maybe he's gotten complacent. Maybe he's satisfied with
the way things are now. Maybe he's not sure I can handle it.
That's great! Now I'm ready, and he's dragging his heels.*

*God, I'm tired of being patient. Amy seems to be doing
well. The kids have accepted me. I learned to cook. What else
do I need to do?*

Her melancholy continued through the reception. She
smiled and greeted people with lips and cheerful words, but
her heart kept reminding her that this was someone else's
wedding. For years she'd shunned the thought of ever being
married, having a family. Now she yearned for Greg to be her
husband, for his children to want her too.

❧

"We're hungry!" Tom and Jake called out from the backseat
in unison.

"How can you be hungry?" asked Greg. "You ate cake and
cookies and nuts and candy at the reception."

"That's not food," declared Thomas.

"I'm hungry too," confessed Caroline.

"Let's go to Mike's Northtown Burgers," suggested Jake.

"Yeah," cheered Tom.

"No," said Greg, "as long as you are dressed up so nice,
let's take Miss Freedman to a nice restaurant."

"Awww," said the two boys.

"I can always take you home," offered Greg.

"No, that's okay. We'll go."

Snickering followed this bit of conversation, and Jane
turned into her seat to look closely at the boys. They both
took their hands, behind which they had been whispering and
snorting, away from their mouths. Expressions of great innocence descended upon their faces, and they turned to look

out the window. As soon as she faced forward, she heard a fresh outbreak of muffled laughter. She looked at Greg. He raised his eyebrows and shrugged. Some things must mystify a father as well.

After they ordered in the restaurant and the food was served, the boys settled down to eat. Jane couldn't help but think something was going on. The children exchanged looks and giggles with no apparent reason. Greg seemed intent on not noticing their odd behavior.

"May I be excused for a minute, Dad?" asked Amy when the waitress cleared dishes and offered dessert.

"Sure, Honey," he answered. "It's near the front entrance."

Now why did that cause an outbreak of suppressed hilarity?

She came back clasping the string handles of a large paper bag. Caroline and the boys sat up straight and still.

"What's this?" asked Jane suspiciously.

"Presents," blurted Tom.

"For you," said Jake.

"It's not my birthday," said Jane.

Amy handed the bag to her father and sat down with a smug smile on her face.

"No," said Greg, "not your birthday. But the children and I have a question to ask you, and we are not above plying you with presents."

Greg reached in and brought out a small velvet jeweler's box. He cleared his throat.

"We talked it over and decided that each of us would pick something to show you our sincerity, our commitment, our hope—"

"Daddy," Caroline whispered impatiently.

"He wants you to marry us," put in Jake.

"*We* want you to marry us," said Tom.

Greg nodded. "Yes, will you marry us, me?"

He opened the box and displayed the diamond solitaire.

Jane felt tears forming behind her eyes, and she steeled herself not to weep in the restaurant. She nodded. Greg slipped the ring on her finger and then kissed her hand where it rested.

"Our presents," demanded Jake.

Greg leaned forward and kissed her quickly before reaching in and pulling out another gift. The flat, ineptly wrapped, flowered paper package had a Christmas bow taped to the top.

"The children picked something from the house to give to you to symbolize that you're welcome. This is from Jacob."

Jane smiled as Jake jumped out of his chair to come stand beside her. She pulled off the paper to find an envelope within. She opened that and pulled out a small piece of paper torn from a kindergarten writing tablet.

"Dump truck." She read the missive. A puzzled frown creased her brow. "You're giving me your dump truck."

Everyone laughed. Jake most of all.

"No," he said through the giggles. "It's the password to the computer. Only the family knows the password. Now you can play games on the computer when you come to live with us."

She gave him a big hug and said her thanks. Greg handed her another package.

"From Thomas," said Greg.

This, too, was a very small package but lumpy. Tom came to stand at her other side squeezing between Jane and his dad. It was a key. Tom threw his arms around her and whispered in her ear. "It's the key to the house."

Jane hugged him back, and again said thank you through the lump in her throat.

The next package, long and skinny with a bump at one end had Caroline's name on it. A wooden spoon.

"*Not* for spankings," she explained. "It's because you're such a good cook now, and you'll be cooking dinner 'cause you'll be our mother."

"What if somebody needs a spanking?" she asked, teasing.

The boys looked at each other and grinned.

"We *never* need spankings."

"Humph!" said their dad and pulled out the last package.

"Scoot," ordered Amy. "I want to sit next to her when she opens my gift."

Caroline gave Jane a hug and whispered in her ear, "You marrying Daddy was what I asked God for when I wished upon Princess." The boys relinquished both their spots, and Amy sat on her father's knee close to Jane.

Jane unwrapped the carefully done package. It was a small painting about the size of a notebook page. In a field, a man and a woman danced in the sunlight. Two boys and two girls romped in the flowered grass around them. Several bare places in the field suggested the picture was not finished yet.

"This is a painting my mom did," Amy explained. "That's Mom and Dad in the center."

Jane nodded. The figures represented Greg and Kathy well.

"These are us. In the painting we're all toddlers. Mom waited until we could walk before she put us in the picture. She said that we would always be her little children no matter how much we grew up."

Again Jane nodded, unable to speak. Her throat closed with emotion, and the words in her mind seemed mired in the same nebulous emotion.

"The empty spaces in the grass were for more family, because Mommy always said our family would be bigger. Now that you're here with us that can happen. If she could, Miss Freedman, she'd paint over herself in the middle and put you dancing with Daddy. She'd probably put herself sitting, watching from under a tree. Maybe that one because it has flowers. She'd think it was all right for you to be in the picture. Honest, she would. She'd like our family to grow."

Tears coursed down Jane's cheeks.

"Thank you, Amy, thank you." Amy and Jane embraced.

"You made her cry, Amy," Jake said accusingly.

Amy patted Jane on the back and held her close.

"It's a girl thing, Jake," Amy said through her own tears. "Don't worry."

"Daddy?" Jake wanted confirmation from a higher authority.

"Yeah, Jake," assured Greg as he beamed into Jane's eyes over Amy's shoulder. "It's a girl thing. Everything's going to be all right."

A Letter To Our Readers

Dear Reader:

In order that we might better contribute to your reading enjoyment, we would appreciate your taking a few minutes to respond to the following questions. We welcome your comments and read each form and letter we receive. When completed, please return to the following:

Rebecca Germany, Fiction Editor
Heartsong Presents
PO Box 719
Uhrichsville, Ohio 44683

1. Did you enjoy reading *Out in the Real World* by Kathleen Paul?
   ❑ Very much! I would like to see more books by this author!
   ❑ Moderately. I would have enjoyed it more if

   _____

   _____

2. Are you a member of **Heartsong Presents**? Yes ❑ No ❑
   If no, where did you purchase this book?_____

   _____

3. How would you rate, on a scale from 1 (poor) to 5 (superior), the cover design?_____

4. On a scale from 1 (poor) to 10 (superior), please rate the following elements.

   _____ Heroine   _____ Plot

   _____ Hero   _____ Inspirational theme

   _____ Setting   _____ Secondary characters

5. These characters were special because_____

   _____

   _____

6. How has this book inspired your life?_____

   _____

   _____

7. What settings would you like to see covered in future
   Heartsong Presents books?_____

   _____

   _____

8. What are some inspirational themes you would like to see
   treated in future books?_____

   _____

   _____

9. Would you be interested in reading other **Heartsong
   Presents** titles?   Yes ❏   No ❏

10. Please check your age range:
    ❏ Under 18   ❏ 18-24   ❏ 25-34
    ❏ 35-45   ❏ 46-55   ❏ Over 55

Name _____

Occupation _____

Address _____

City _____ State _____ Zip _____

Email _____